THEIR MOMENT OF HAPPINESS

A PRIDE & PREJUDICE VARIATION

LUCY MARIN

Quills & Quartos
PUBLISHING

Edited by Debra Anne Watson and Jan Ashton

Cover Design by Susan Adriani, CloudCat Design

ISBN 978-1-967030-46-0 (ebook) and 978-1-967030-47-7 (paperback)

To Jane Austen, in gratitude

CONTENTS

PROLOGUE

London, October 1812

Margaret Fitzwilliam, the Countess of Romsley, sat on a sofa in her townhouse, staring at her sister-in-law, Lady Catherine de Bourgh, who was delivering a tirade. The woman had intruded on what had been a perfectly ordinary morning. The earl and she had only just finished breakfast. Their elder son, Viscount Bramwell, had not yet made an appearance, and their younger, Colonel Fitzwilliam was at an early meeting, having expected to return in time for the meal, but he had not. *If only he was here! We could use as many rational heads present as possible.*

What was particularly astonishing—and, truth be told, perplexing—was her sister's insistence that they immediately depart London and go to Hertfordshire to prevent 'a monumental disaster'.

"Darcy will be the ruin of us all!" Catherine said loudly.

"Darcy—" Romsley attempted to interject, but his sister spoke on, her volume increasing.

"Despite being engaged to my daughter, I have heard from more than one reliable source that he intends to propose marriage to another girl!"

"Darcy and Anne are engaged?" the earl asked. "Why is this the first I am learning of it?"

"Where *is* Anne?" Margaret said.

Catherine addressed her question first. "Resting." She then scowled at her brother and said, "When he was at Rosings at Easter, we spoke of the wedding being this autumn. There is no need to make a big to-do about an engagement when we have known they would marry since they were in their cradles."

The earl and countess exchanged a look, silently confirming that neither of them had heard that their niece and nephew would marry that autumn, and it *was* already October. But she had no time to consider the matter further; it was more important to attend to Catherine's explanation of why she was so alarmed.

"The entire family expects their union. Everyone in our social circle expects it. My daughter expects it!" Catherine insisted. "Is she to be thrown over after waiting years for him to finally be ready to settle down?"

"Has he proposed to Anne, yes or no?" the earl interjected.

Fixing her eyes on her brother, Catherine said, "They have spoken of it, yes."

"Then he cannot possibly be on the point of proposing to another lady," Margaret replied, shaking her head.

With a loud scoff, Catherine said, "Lady? She is no such thing. That girl has tricked him, used her arts and allurements to make him forget his duty. It is up to *us* to remind him." Jabbing a finger at Romsley, she added, "You, especially, as the head of the family."

She then stood and began to pace, her walking stick striking the floor heavily with each step. The countess, long convinced the other woman had no need of the instrument, wished she would put it down. *I believe she only carries it so she might shake it at people, making herself look ridiculous.*

"Darcy acknowledges that it was the dearest wish of his parents," Catherine continued. "It was their intention —as well as that of my husband and I—that they would unite the two families. My brother-in-law and I were writing of it in the months before he died, discussing the marriage contract, the timing of the wedding, what renovations were needed at Pemberley. Darcy is bound to my daughter!"

"But who is this girl you think he—?" The earl's question remained unfinished when his sister spoke over him.

"Elizabeth Bennet," she hissed through clenched teeth. For several minutes, she shared everything she knew of the young woman, beginning with having met her when she had stayed at the parsonage near Rosings the previous spring. "I knew I should have insisted Mr Collins send her away. She seemed like a prettyish sort of girl, the usual country chit of no account, when I first met her. As soon as my nephews arrived, her true character emerged. You ought to have seen her! Shamelessly flirting with them, especially Darcy, once she marked him as the better catch. I warned him she would do whatever was necessary to ensnare him, but he dismissed my concerns. It was too well known that he was promised to Anne for any other girl to suppose he would take an interest in her." She made a noise of disgust and vexation.

Speaking as delicately as possible, Margaret asked, "Is it possible Darcy has changed his mind? If there is no formal engagement and no marriage contract between him and Anne..."

Catherine stopped pacing and stared at her, her stick aloft and pointed in the countess's direction. "I told you Hugh Darcy and I were writing of it when he died. He, along with my sister, meant for their son to marry Anne. How many times must I say it? I have proof—letters we exchanged in which we discussed our children's union in detail. There can be no doubt of his father's wishes. If he were alive, he would insist his son fulfil his obligation to my daughter and this family. Since he is not, *you* will do it." She used the walking stick to indicate her brother. Margaret knew this was more likely to annoy than convince him.

With an enviable calmness, he said, "Did you show Darcy these letters? Do you have them with you now?"

She waved her hand impatiently. "They are in Kent. My word that they exist is good enough. Darcy is aware of what his parents wanted for him, and he was prepared to see to it—until his head was turned by this girl. It is not to be borne!"

"Catherine," she said, "if he genuinely cares for this other girl—"

"Darcy is far too rational to fall for a chit like that unless there was some devilry at work. And even if he did, marrying her would tarnish his reputation irreparably, to say nothing of what it would do to my daughter and the rest of us. Elizabeth Bennet has no fortune, no proper education, and her mother's people are from trade. One of the uncles lives in the city, in sight of his warehouses! As if that were not shocking enough, her youngest sister, barely fifteen years old, has recently eloped with George Wickham, the son of Pemberley's former steward!"

Fortunately, Catherine did not know that their own niece had nearly eloped with the same man the previous summer. Recalling Georgiana's severe agitation and knowing what it would have meant for her and the family—both Fitzwilliams and Darcys—had it not been prevented, made Margaret miss a moment or two of her sister-in-law's speech. She did not need to hear it, however, to guess at its content. How could Darcy possibly call Mr Wickham his brother? What would that do to Georgiana? Her husband squeezed her hand; no doubt his thoughts had moved along the same path as hers.

"To say nothing of the scandal!" Catherine began to pace again. "Her father tried to patch it up, but everyone knows the girl eloped, actually lived with him unmarried for days—*weeks*—and that they are married now does not erase it. Can you imagine the gossip if our nephew were to tie himself to such a family? As if making such an imprudent choice were not bad enough, he would marry into a disgraceful family, and—worst of all—he would be jilting Anne! My daughter, the granddaughter of an earl, could never show her face in town again. Will you allow this to happen? Think of Bramwell and Fitzwilliam, neither of whom are married. Which is another matter we must discuss, and we shall, once this business with Darcy is settled. It is past time for Bramwell and Lady Cassandra to marry."

In addition to Darcy and Anne's union, the family had long anticipated a match between Bramwell and the daughter of one of the earl's closest political allies. With reluctance, the countess recognised that her sister-in-law had a point; at thirty, her eldest son should settle.

Romsley shook his head. "Darcy cannot do this. Even if he has not made a formal offer to Anne, it seems he has agreed to the arrangement. Besides, he cannot possibly marry a penniless country girl with ties to trade, especially one whose family is embroiled in scandal."

Pressing a hand to her chest, Margaret said, "I hate the thought that he is being deceived, that he will be heartbroken when he discovers he has been tricked into proposing."

The earl tightened his grip on her hand, and the conversation shifted to how they would act. Her husband said he would send an express to Darcy, demanding he return to London, but he soon agreed with his sister that it would be better to go to Hertfordshire. They would give their nephew no warning, lest that encourage him to hasten making his proposal, which it likely would, especially if he told the girl of his family's concerns.

Arrangements were quickly made, and Anne recalled from the chamber in which she had been resting. They were gathered in the drawing room, waiting to be told the coach was ready, when Bramwell and Fitzwilliam joined them. Fitzwilliam greeted them and apologised for missing breakfast. Bramwell yawned, his brow furrowing as he regarded his aunt and cousin.

"What is happening?" he enquired.

The earl explained, Catherine interrupting several times.

Fitzwilliam was incredulous. "*Darcy* is going to make an unsuitable marriage?"

"We are going to prevent it!" Catherine said, her voice harsh.

"That does not sound like my cousin," Bramwell said. "There must be some sort of misunderstanding." He gave his aunt a sidelong glance, subtly suggesting *she* was the source of it.

The countess could not entirely disagree, but it was vitally important to take the utmost care when selecting a marriage partner, and she was worried her nephew had not. It was as well they were going to find out for themselves what his intentions were. *And there is the matter of Anne and his obligation to her.*

Romsley said, "If there is, we shall soon discover it.

But if even half of what my sister says about this girl and her family is true, Darcy will not marry her, especially when it means he would be disappointing Anne. If he does, he will face severe consequences."

The brothers looked at each other and said, almost as one, "We are coming with you!"

CHAPTER ONE

Hertfordshire

Darcy glanced at the beautiful lady walking by his side. His heart was so full of longing and hope—desperate, aching hope—that it had pushed all thought from him, robbing him of his ability to speak. When last he had seen Elizabeth Bennet, whom he had loved for the better part of a year, her silence towards him had been enough to convince him that she could never return his love, could not even esteem him sufficiently to marry him. But then his meddlesome aunt had called on him in London, and what she had said gave him reason to believe his dearest wish might come true. Elizabeth had refused to promise Lady Catherine that she would never accept his proposal.

Why can I not speak? He berated himself for stupidity; had he not spent hours, literally hours, practising what he would say? He did not want to make a fool of himself and insult her as he had the previous spring in Kent. Yet at present, being so close to her that he could smell the light floral scent she wore, he was speechless.

The day was fair, and they, Bingley, Miss Bennet, and Miss Catherine had set out on a walk. The younger lady had just left them, skipping down the lane towards Lucas Lodge, and the other couple, lately betrothed, were some ways behind him and Elizabeth. It was the perfect time for him to ask if her feelings for him had improved, if she could forgive him for not making Wickham's evilness known earlier, which might have prevented her sister Lydia's elopement and eventual marriage to the scoundrel.

At the very moment he was prepared to slap himself to dislodge the words stuck in his throat, she—his wonderful, beautiful Elizabeth—thanked him for his efforts to secure her sister's reputation. He thrust aside disappointment that Mrs Gardiner had told her about his involvement and seized his opportunity.

"You are too generous to trifle with me. If your feelings are still what they were last April, tell me so at once. My affections and wishes are unchanged, but one word from you will silence me on the subject for ever."

His heart thudded so loudly, he was afraid he would not be able to hear her response. Eagerly observing her, he noticed signs of embarrassment. Her cheeks were pink, which made him want to caress and kiss them before turning his attention to her lips. They were presently twitching as though she was trying not to smile, or was attempting to form words, or possibly both. Her eyes, bright and expressive as always, briefly met his.

And then she did smile—a broad, marvellous grin full of promise and joy, and an expression of heartfelt delight diffused over her face. She opened her mouth and softly, so tenderly, she said, "Mr Darcy, I—"

"Mr Darcy! Sir, oh, I'm glad to have found you!"

Darcy turned towards the most unexpected and unwanted intruder. Rushing towards them was a youthful footman named John he recognised as belonging to Netherfield. The man was flushed, and he breathed heavily, as though he had been running. Darcy wanted to scream and possibly kick him for interrupting at just that moment, just when he was about to secure his future happiness.

"What is it?" he asked, battling between frustration and knowing the man would not have sought him out if the matter was not serious.

"Sir, your family has arrived. At Netherfield Park, I mean." He paused and pressed a hand to his chest as he evidently sought to control his breathing.

"My family?" Darcy's brow furrowed as he regarded the footman, then Elizabeth. She stepped closer to him, her features displaying the anxiety he felt.

John nodded. "There must be half a dozen of them, sir. They demanded to see you at once, and were not pleased to hear you were not there. The butler sent me to find you."

Again, Darcy looked at Elizabeth. She grasped his hand,

likely supposing as he did that something grave must have occurred for his relations to travel to Hertfordshire without warning. A multitude of questions ran through his mind: Who had come? Was Georgiana with them? Had something happened to his sister, or had someone died? But why would they not just send an express to inform him?

"You must go," Elizabeth said. She nodded, which he took as her way of saying all was well between them.

"Come with me. Please," he said. "Whatever has happened…" If it was dreadful news, he would be able to confront it better with her by his side.

"Of course," she replied at once.

Her hand was still in his, and he tightened his grip to communicate his gratitude. Looking behind him, he saw that Bingley and Miss Bennet were not so far away; their pace had quickened, no doubt because of the footman's arrival.

"Bingley, some of my relations—I do not know which —have come to see me. I-I do not know why," Darcy called.

Miss Bennet's eyes widened, and she covered her mouth with her gloved hand. Bingley's shock and concern were equally as visible. He said, "Go. I shall…" His gaze went to Miss Bennet and then Elizabeth.

"I will return with him," Elizabeth said, giving her sister a resolute, reassuring smile.

"We shall join you there. You are much faster walkers than I am," Miss Bennet said.

Darcy nodded and turned his steps towards the path leading to Netherfield. On his own, he might have run, but it was worth the extra time it would take to have Elizabeth with him.

"What could it mean?" he said, more to himself than her. "What if something has happened to Georgiana?"

"I know you do not expect me to answer, but surely we shall find our fears are for naught. If something terrible had happened, your family would have sent an express, asking you to go to London or wherever you were needed."

Her hand was still in his, and he was tempted to kiss it; probably he would have, if it had not meant slowing their pace. "I have thought the same. But it is very odd."

"We shall find out what has brought them here soon enough. I am certain all will be well."

He nodded, struggling to believe her. *But as long as I have her love, I can confront any challenge, no matter how dreadful.*

CHAPTER TWO

Entering Netherfield, the butler directed Darcy and Elizabeth to the drawing room. Once there, he took in the various people arranged in seats or standing near the fireplace. He had not known what to anticipate, and seeing his aunt and uncle, the Earl and Countess of Romsley, and their two sons, along with Lady Catherine and her daughter Anne, was shocking, incongruous, although he felt he had no right to the sensation. He regarded them with trepidation, an icy sensation forming deep in his stomach.

"What—" he said, unable to finish his question as Lady Catherine spoke over him, insisting, "She has no business here. You will leave at once!"

Darcy's gaze followed his aunt's finger to discover she was pointing at Elizabeth. Her rudeness ought not to be a surprise. She had made her disdain for Elizabeth plain. He met his beloved's bright eyes and gave her a brief head shake to communicate his desire that she remain regardless of what anyone else said.

To his aunt, he said, "Miss Elizabeth has every reason to be here, if only because I wish it." Turning to her again, he quickly named his other relations so that she would know who was present beyond the three she had previously met: Lady Catherine and his cousins Anne de Bourgh and Colonel Fitzwilliam. To his family, he asked, "Why are you here?" His panic, which had momentarily been masked by irritation with Lady Catherine, returned, and not allowing anyone the opportunity to speak, he added, "Has something happened to Georgiana?"

Fitzwilliam shook his head and said, "No."

His voice was nearly lost behind Lady Catherine's louder, more strident tone. "We are here to demand you end your connexion to that girl and her family once and for all." Again, she thrust a finger in Elizabeth's direction; he wanted to slap it away. "I never would have believed that you, my own nephew, would be so stubborn, so intractable as you were when we last spoke in town. Your unwillingness to see past that girl's arts and allurements, to remember your duty to your family, to your own dear parents' wishes! I am ashamed of you."

"This is ridiculous!" Darcy interjected.

Lord Romsley took a step away from the fireplace and towards Darcy. "Do not speak to your aunt in that manner!"

"What of her manner of speaking to Miss Elizabeth, to say nothing of me?" Darcy retorted.

Bramwell leant against the mantel; he appeared to

snigger. Lady Romsley held a handkerchief to her mouth. Beside her on a sofa was Anne; as always, she only seemed to be partly attending to the conversation. Fitzwilliam, who had been nearest to Lady Catherine, stood and went to his brother.

"Neither of you was willing to do what is right, what self-interest and the dictates of society, of responsibility to one's family and future generations, demand," Lady Catherine went on, apparently willing to overlook whatever else was said. "Thus, you have forced my hand. You will marry my daughter this autumn."

Darcy felt like knocking his head against the wall. *Though, it might be better to do it to my aunt. Dislodge this nonsense and allow sense to take its place.* "There is nothing you can say to convince me to give into your desire—"

"Not just mine," his aunt interrupted with an air of triumph. "It was your mother's fondest wish and your father's intention that you unite the Darcy and de Bourgh estates. I have proof of it. He wrote to me shortly before his death. We were preparing the marriage contract."

In London, Lady Catherine had attempted to browbeat him into succumbing to her demands, while in the next breath, she had informed him of Elizabeth's refusal to say that she would never accept an offer of marriage from him. He recalled wanting to laugh at his aunt; at the very moment she had given him hope that he might yet claim the woman he loved with everything that he was, she wanted him to agree to marry a lady he barely liked, let alone held in tender regard.

Darcy slowly shook his head, unsure what to say, and not entirely certain any of this was real. Was it all a dream, from proposing to Elizabeth to his family's nonsensical intrusion?

The countess said, "Can you not see how this situation is distressing poor Anne?"

It was unclear which situation she meant, although Anne did look uneasy. Her head was lowered, and she was twisting a linen handkerchief in her hands. From what Darcy had been able to discern over the years, his cousin would be willing to become his wife, but who was to say whether it was her wish or if she was only doing what she believed to be her duty?

"Listen to your aunts, Darcy," the earl demanded.

He heard a heavy sigh from the direction of his male cousins, but he did not know which of them had made the noise. Glancing at Elizabeth, he could not fail to notice signs of shock. She stood still, and he saw her swallow heavily. Frustration and anger at his family burned in his stomach, and along with it, fear of her reaction. What if she decided she did not want to come between him and his family? What if this disgusting scene reminded her of the ill-advised, hurtful words he had said during their disastrous interview in Kent? Why had the footman not been delayed even a minute? Then she would have accepted him, they would be betrothed—leaving aside the need for her father's permission—and nothing that was happening presently could threaten to separate them; both he and Elizabeth would be bound by honour, as well as mutual affection. As surreptitiously as possible, he brushed his finger against her hand and was rewarded by her looking at him. She gave him a smile—almost too slight to see, but it meant everything.

For now, I shall allow my aunt to say what she likes. Then I shall send her on her way, along with my other relations, after making them understand that I am my own man and no duty requires me to live my life as they want me to! There was no purpose to entering into a screaming match with Lady Catherine. It might distress Elizabeth, and certainly would Lady Romsley and Anne. It would also be against his nature, and he knew it would have displeased his mother to see him treating her sister with less than respect. Briefly, he wondered if his mother—and father—would approve of her treating him as she was.

"Anne and I understood young men need time," Lady Catherine went on. "With your father's death, we grudgingly accepted that another delay was necessary, although it would have comforted you to have a devoted wife by your side."

This time, the snigger that came from his cousins' direction was loud enough that both Bramwell and Fitzwilliam must have contributed to it. Lady Romsley turned in their direction, giving them what Darcy supposed was a reprimanding look.

"Anne then had that unfortunate setback with her health, but she is better now," Lady Catherine said.

"None of this materially alters the situation, madam," Darcy interjected. "Not a week ago, I told you, as plainly as possible, that I am *not* willing to marry Anne. Nothing you say will alter my feelings on the matter. I will not be swayed by the notion of adding Rosings to my wealth or because you and my mother dreamt of your children marrying one day."

Lady Catherine's eyes narrowed. "You are much mistaken if you believe you can so easily toss aside all the plans your parents have made for you. I have not been in the habit of brooking disappointment. You and Anne are formed for each other. Your parents and hers intended for the match to take place—as you well know—and it will!"

Darcy ran a hand over his mouth before responding, hoping to keep himself from saying anything that would be cruel or needlessly insulting, such as that his life would become one of misery if he succumbed to her demands. Most of all, he did not want to draw attention to Elizabeth by comparing her to his cousin. There was not a man in England who would prefer Anne de Bourgh to Elizabeth Bennet—unless they were sorely in need of Anne's wealth. Miss Bennet and Bingley had quietly entered the room, and Darcy did not want either of them, or Elizabeth, to have to witness him having a fit of ill-temper. *But it would relieve some of my fury if I could hit or throw something!*

He said, "Yet, neither my father nor my mother ever spoke to me of this arrangement you claim was so dear to you all." If he were being completely honest, this was a slight prevarication. His mother had died when he was thirteen years old, and he did not recall her ever mentioning his future marriage. But his father had made a few casual remarks about it; he might even have mentioned Anne, but it had been years ago, and Darcy was not certain. He had not paid much attention, being too young to contemplate such matters. When he turned one-and-twenty, his father had said that he should amuse himself for several years—until he was five- or six-and-twenty—and that then they would 'see to things'. With his father's sudden death two years later, they had never had a chance to discuss marriage or his father's hopes further.

Darcy turned to Elizabeth and added, "I will make my own decisions, as is my right."

"Not regarding this matter," Lord Romsley said, his gaze steady on Elizabeth. His look was one of disapproval, and it left Darcy determined to find out what he had been told about her and by whom, although he could guess the answer. If his uncle took even five minutes to know her, his objections would lessen.

"You will marry Anne," Lady Catherine said for what seemed the tenth time in the last few minutes. Her voice became menacing as she continued. "Or you will risk a scandal that will ruin you. Your entire family will turn against you."

"I doubt that," Darcy said. His aunt could be vindictive, but, in the end, there was not much she could do to damage him, and his family was too sensible to break with him. It was not as though he intended to marry a scullery maid; Elizabeth was a gentleman's daughter. "For the last time, there is no engagement, you—"

"There is!" Lady Catherine cried.

"I believe it is time for Jane and me to depart," Elizabeth said, her tone deceptively calm.

Instantly, Darcy forgot about everyone else; all his attention was on her. Something he could not name told him the consequences of her leaving, of allowing this appalling conversation with his relations to continue, would be dire. He lightly grasped her elbow. "No! It is not necessary. I shall tell them—"

"Let her go, Darcy," Lord Romsley said. "This is a family matter, and we shall settle it amongst ourselves."

At the same moment, Lady Catherine said, "The chit finally says something worth hearing!"

Elizabeth did not look at either of them, and he saw a flash of anger in her eyes before she lowered her gaze, apparently no longer willing or able to regard him either. Her posture stiffened, and he would not be surprised if she literally bit her tongue to avoid retorting. Softly, she said, "I must. The earl is correct that this is for you to-to…resolve."

She stepped away from him, and he watched as she reached for Miss Bennet's hand and, together, they continued to the door.

His expression one of sympathy and support, Bingley said, "I shall arrange my carriage for them. Leave you to…"

He followed the ladies from the room, and Darcy turned to once again do battle with his exceedingly obstinate, bull-headed, interfering aunt.

Elizabeth was too dazed to think. She walked out of Netherfield mechanically, separating herself from Jane and Mr Bingley while they waited for his carriage. There was a stone bench at a slight remove, and she sat there, staring ahead of her, willing herself to shake off the fog of confusion that enveloped her.

What had just happened? She had been so glad to learn that Mr Darcy had returned! Although she would not allow herself to fully believe it meant he still cared for her and would renew his addresses, the look he had given her when they first met again that morning suggested that he did love her. It was difficult to describe the difference, but when he had come to the neighbourhood with Mr Bingley the previous month, his demeanour had been cautious; his silence had convinced her that Lydia's elopement represented an insurmountable barrier between them. But today, his expression had been one of determination and warmth, and it had left her almost sick with anticipated joy.

Then, just as she was about to assure him that she loved him and longed to be his wife, they had been interrupted. That had been unexpected, to be sure, but she had never considered that the footman approaching them meant the start of her dreams of a happy future with Mr Darcy crumbling down about her. That had happened once before, in the Lambton Inn when she had told him of Jane's letter announcing Lydia's rash actions. But at present, her expectations had been so much higher!

He said that he still loves me, still wants to marry me.

And, oh, how I want that too! He cannot be engaged to his cousin!

Willing—needing—to believe Mr Darcy was too honourable to pursue her if he had even the slightest obligation to Miss de Bourgh, Elizabeth leant against the warm stone of the house, closed her eyes, and forced her mind to be still. She would return home and, as much as it was possible, wait patiently for him to call and explain the scene she had just witnessed. Later today, or at the latest the next morning, he would come to her, tell her his relations were gone, and they would laugh about it.

She sighed. While she anticipated seeing him soon and learning what was behind his family's unexpected visit, she doubted even she would be able to find humour in the episode.

"Our moment of happiness has been ruined," she whispered. "It was so close, almost within our grasp and then..." The great fireball of joy inside of her had been ready to burst, filling her with a warmth and contentment she knew would last a lifetime. Instead, Lady Catherine, the odious woman, had come to wreak havoc. When she had been at Longbourn and Elizabeth had refused to promise she would never marry Mr Darcy, the woman had said she knew how to act, and apparently she did. Elizabeth could only pray the damage she did was of short duration.

CHAPTER THREE

Although Darcy's inclination was to follow Elizabeth from the room and apologise for his family's unconscionable behaviour, he did not. Instead, he glared at his uncle and aunts in turn, overlooking the combined expressions of sympathy and amusement on his male cousins' faces and Anne's sniffling.

Lady Catherine expressed satisfaction that Elizabeth was gone, adding, "Without her disruptive presence, we can turn our minds to more important matters. You and Anne will be married from Rosings, as is appropriate. It is her home, after all."

"Anne and I will not be married anywhere," Darcy stated, wondering if he was going mad. Or perhaps he had suffered a grave injury that had left him unconscious, capable of hearing people speaking about him but unable to voice his responses. Surely there must be some extraordinary explanation for why they did not understand his refusal.

"Do you think Mr Bingley minds us invading his house in this manner?" Bramwell said. The non sequitur caused everyone to look in his direction, which was likely his cousin's purpose in speaking. Bramwell affected a large yawn. That, in itself, was not too rude—for him, at least—but the pointed way he was regarding Lady Catherine was a bit much.

"Bramwell, that is enough," Lord Romsley said, while at the same time, Lady Romsley said, "Oh, Bramwell, now is not the moment for your levity."

"My brother does raise an interesting point, however," Fitzwilliam remarked. "We have arrived without notice, and it is hardly the thing to take over the principal room of another man's house to sort out family affairs."

"We shall not remain," Lady Catherine said. "Darcy, order your man to pack your things. We shall depart for Rosings as soon as it is done."

Darcy gaped at her. What had he ever done since becoming an adult to make her believe he would obey her demands? Raising his voice slightly, he said, "I am not going to Kent. Indeed, after how you spoke to me in London and your behaviour today, I can assure you, your ladyship, that it will be a very long time before I set foot inside Rosings again. If I ever do!"

"Do not be ridiculous," she retorted. Behind her voice, Darcy heard both the earl's and countess's, though he was not sure what they said. "You will be master of Rosings, just as your parents and Sir Lewis and I intended. Naturally, you must spend a good part of the year there to ensure it is properly managed. It is your duty, both to the estate and your second son, who will inherit it. We shall divide our time thus. Four months in Derbyshire, four months in Kent, and four months in town and visiting others."

We? he silently thought. Did the woman expect to accompany Anne and her husband wherever they went? If she did, she was mad. What man always wanted his mother-in-law nearby? *Not that she will ever hold that position in my life.* Anne would never be his wife. The only lady he would ever make Mrs Darcy was Elizabeth. Although he had resolved such before this morning, each word his aunt spoke added to his determination and reminded him why Elizabeth was the perfect lady for him.

Taking a fortifying breath, Darcy said, "I am growing fatigued of repeating myself. I shall not waste my breath telling you what you ought to know already. The only people travelling to Kent today are you, Lady Catherine, and your daughter. I shall have your carriage—"

"Not so hasty!" she interjected.

"Enough," the earl said. Darcy suspected he had used the word more today than he usually did in a month. "Netherfield is not the best venue for discussing such an important family matter. We shall go to town. There, we can sort this out. Catherine, your demands are only antagonising my nephew. Once we are in London, I shall speak to him, and since he is a reasonable man—and I know my sister and brother-in-law raised him to respect his heritage—he will accept his duty and live up to the promises he made his cousin."

Dear Lord, please let me wake up now! Darcy screamed to himself. He pressed his eyes closed, willing himself to believe that when he opened them, his family would have disappeared. Unfortunately, they had not. Fitzwilliam's expression had grown more apologetic—even though he had done nothing to require an apology, as far as Darcy knew—and sympathetic, while his brother's features now suggested more irritation than amusement. Anne continued to dab at her nose, now and again looking about her as if she had no notion where she was or why. His three older relations stared at him, appearing to await his next words.

"I refuse to continue this conversation. Prepare to depart. I will *not* be going with you."

Lady Catherine's voice was like ice. "You will do as I say, or I shall not only ruin you, I shall ruin that chit and her family."

"Your union to her is impossible," the earl added. "Give up the notion or face the consequences."

Fury roared in Darcy's ears, masking whatever his uncle and aunts were saying; he knew they spoke by the motion of their lips. He wanted to scream, to lambast them fiercely for destroying the beautiful moment he and Elizabeth had been on the point of having, and for their indefensible actions and lack of respect for her and for him. Even after the dispute was resolved, his connexion to them would be damaged, perhaps forever.

Bramwell strode towards him, soon closing the distance. He grabbed Darcy's arm and pulled him to the door, saying, "I think that is quite enough for the moment. No one, not even our aunt, wants to see the family torn to bits and tossed in the rubbish heap, as it surely will be if we do not all cool our tempers before continuing the discussion."

Darcy sensed Fitzwilliam behind them, but did not turn to look at him. Rather, he pulled his arm from Bramwell's and immediately sought the door that led to the gardens.

———

The stone bench on which Elizabeth presently sat still retained some of the chill from the previous night. She wished Mr Bingley's carriage would soon make an appearance so that she and Jane might return to Longbourn. Her sister and Mr Bingley stood a little way away, speaking earnestly and glancing at her repeatedly. Neither of them had known that Elizabeth and Mr Darcy were...well, that they were anything other than indifferent acquaintances.

The strangest sensations battled inside of her, and it left her dizzy and nauseous. It had begun in the Netherfield drawing room and must be a combination of shock, confusion, and devastation. At the moment, she could not make sense of what had happened. Was there some proof that Mr Darcy—*her* Mr Darcy—was, in fact, bound to his cousin Miss de Bourgh? But then, if it were so, he would not be her Mr Darcy; he would just be Mr Darcy, her soon-to-be brother's dearest friend.

"Just a few more seconds and I would have accepted

his proposal," she softly murmured, her lips barely moving. Would it have made a difference? Could it have been used to stop his family's insistence that he was obligated to marry Miss de Bourgh? She doubted it, not when there had been no announcement, not even an application for her father's consent.

Before long, she decided to join her sister, anticipating the carriage would soon be there. She stopped some steps away from the lately-engaged couple.

When Jane noticed her, she started and cried, "Oh, Lizzy, I did not see—" She blushed and glanced at Mr Bingley, her expression begging his assistance in dealing with the awkward scene.

Heat crept into Elizabeth's cheeks, and suddenly, she wished she had confided in Jane, been more open about what had taken place in Lambton, from seeing the Bingleys and Darcys and, crucially, of her changing feelings for Mr Darcy. *And how I cried bitter tears the last morning I saw him there, for poor, stupid Lydia, the possible devastating consequences for our family, and because I knew then that I loved him and had lost his good opinion forever.* Or so she had thought until this very day when he had once again proposed.

Fortunately, she was not required to speak immediately. The carriage arrived, and Elizabeth almost leapt inside as soon as the steps were lowered. She was eager to be home again so that she might be alone. Mr Bingley took a seat opposite her and Jane, the first indication she had that he intended to go to Longbourn with them.

Once on their way for the short journey, she sensed

Jane's eyes on her, but she kept her own gaze firmly fixed on the view from the window. Attempting not to draw her sister's notice, Elizabeth surreptitiously shook her head, hoping to dispel a portion of her bafflement. She wanted, needed, to think rationally, to make sense of what she had witnessed at Netherfield, but that was impossible when what she most felt was that her heart had been ripped from her body. She had experienced something akin to this when she had said goodbye to Mr Darcy in Lambton after telling him about the news she had just received, but this was much, much worse because she had only just allowed herself to accept how deeply she loved him, how essential he was to her happiness, and that he felt the same about her when he proposed earlier this morning.

Mr Bingley broke the silence, saying, "I thought I ought to accompany you. It seemed best to give Darcy and his relations a little time to..." He chuckled awkwardly and looked at Jane, likely hoping she knew what to say to Elizabeth.

Elizabeth simply nodded. Jane took her hand, and she permitted it, despite wishing she could hide from them. She hated being the object of their pity, and, to avoid seeing the emotion in their eyes, she kept her gaze on the window and watched the passing landscape during the short ride. The earlier melange of emotions she had felt settled into a heavy weight in her belly that was pulling her ever downward. She had felt the same once before, although in a less stark manner. It had been just after the death of her beloved grandmother when she had been ten. She supposed this was—or might be—another loss, one that was so much worse. Had she lost her chance to marry Mr Darcy? Was it possible he was legally or morally obligated to his cousin? He was an honourable man, truly the best man she had ever known. His actions regarding Lydia were proof enough, but she could name other reasons to support her belief. If Lady Catherine or his other relations provided evidence that his union to Miss de Bourgh was more than just the fanciful wish of their mothers, he might agree and marry her out of a sense of duty, despite loving Elizabeth.

I do not understand why Miss de Bourgh or her mother would want that, however. To know that he intended to marry another lady, that he loved and desired another lady, yet be content to force him into a union he had rejected was unimaginable to Elizabeth. How did they expect it to end? Surely not in a prosperous, joy-filled marriage of two compatible people who were devoted to each other's happiness and well-being and to building a good life together. That was what Elizabeth wanted of marriage and what she believed she and Mr Darcy would have. All the de Bourgh ladies—and apparently the earl and countess—cared for was how proper the match appeared; they thought only of wealth and connexions, dismissing other considerations.

"Lizzy," Jane said, her voice full of tenderness, "are you well? W-what— You and Mr Darcy, are you—"

"Please, I beg of you, do not ask me about him or what you saw this morning. I can tell you nothing," she interjected, keeping her head averted. Softly, she added, "I cannot speak of it."

"How can you ask me not to?" Jane said. Her voice sounded thick, as though she was close to crying. "Not when I see that you suffer! Liz—"

Once again, Elizabeth interjected. "I admit my feelings for him have changed, but there is nothing else to say of the matter. I cannot explain what happened at Netherfield. Please, Jane—*please*—do not speak of it. Not now."

Jane sighed, but she kept her thoughts to herself. She rested her hand on Elizabeth's arm, and they passed the remainder of the journey thus, only the sounds of the wheels intruding on the silence.

Once at Longbourn, Elizabeth retreated to her chamber with the intention of not leaving it again that day. She threw off her pelisse and bonnet, and sat at the window, which was open an inch or two to let in the breeze, hoping the fresh air would stop the throbbing in her head. Tears filled her eyes, and her breathing became laboured. Afraid of being seen by her younger sisters, who were presently wandering through the gardens below her chamber, she lay on her bed instead, staring at the ceiling, her eyes tracing a thin crack that ran almost the entire length of the room.

"Here I am, alone yet again, desperately seeking hope that somehow this situation will end better than it seems possible at the moment, that somehow Mr Darcy and I will have our happily ever after."

Once far enough from the house, Darcy rounded on his cousins and demanded, "What the devil are you doing here? Did you know what your parents intended to do, what Lady Catherine's purpose was? You cannot agree with them!"

Bramwell grinned. "I thought I might as well join their merry party as not. London has been rather flat of late."

"What with his lady love still in the country. She does not return for a few days." Fitzwilliam sniggered. The remark earned him a punch on the arm from his brother.

Darcy did not know there was a lady his cousin was pursuing. It was not all that surprising, however; the viscount's past included several *affaires de cœur*, but Darcy did not believe any of the ladies had left their mark on his heart. He supposed this time would be no different.

"I do not care about Bramwell's romantic escapades," he said.

Bramwell clutched his chest as though wounded.

Darcy continued, "Were you aware of this... madness?" He indicated the house with a jerk of his thumb.

Speaking at the same time, Fitzwilliam said, "No," and his brother said, "Yes." They regarded each other and, in unison, added, "Not entirely."

Darcy nearly roared with frustration. He counted the

pair amongst his closest friends, but, currently, he despised them. How could they be so flippant?

The colonel suggested they walk, and, as they did, he explained. "We did not even know that our aunt and cousin were in London, and only learnt that they were and that they and our parents intended to come to Hertfordshire this morning. All that we heard was that you were on the point of doing something exceedingly foolish that would ruin your future, bring shame to the family, and I do not know what other doom."

"We decided at once that we should come along," Bramwell said. "Knowing the dragon of Kent, as we all have the misfortune of doing, there was a high probability that what she really meant was that you were not behaving as she wanted. I do not know what she said to the earl and countess, but, evidently, they believed there was sufficient reason for concern to go along with her scheme."

Darcy seethed; his jaw was clenched so tightly that his muscles ached. "What right do any of them have to direct *my* choices, *my* life?"

Bramwell guffawed, and Fitzwilliam said, "Whether they have it or not, we all know they believe they do, thus the scene we were forced to endure. I wish we could have warned you, but we did not know what was going to happen until it was too late to do so." He stopped, momentarily taking hold of Darcy's arm to halt his steps too and asked, "Are you truly interested in marrying Elizabeth Bennet?"

Darcy was not so lost to his anger to miss the surprise

in his cousin's voice. In response, he nodded, keeping his gaze fixed on Fitzwilliam to see how he took the news.

"Are you engaged to her? Have you proposed?" the colonel said.

His mouth went dry, and he felt like he would vomit. How close he had come to being able to answer in the affirmative! He glanced at Bramwell, who appeared calm and curious but not disapproving. At length, Darcy admitted, "She was on the point of accepting me when the servant interrupted and said I was needed at Netherfield. He was so urgent, I was certain something dreadful had happened."

The viscount gave a bark of laughter. "It did, from what I can tell. This girl cannot be so objectionable. What is wrong with her? Oh, trust me"—he paused and shook his head, eyes rolling dramatically— "Lady Catherine had a great deal to say of her and not a word of it good, but I no more believe her than I would that men could fly like the birds." It was likely no coincidence that a flock of birds passed overhead, their black silhouettes stark against the blue sky.

Rather than answer, Darcy looked at Fitzwilliam, his expression challenging. "You have met her. How would you respond?"

The colonel sighed and ran a hand over his mouth. "That she is a charming young lady, lively, witty, very pretty. Not the sort of girl I would expect you would find attractive, given how she liked to vex you. And that she has no connexions, no money, has not been brought up with the expectations of our social sphere, and thus, is doubly not the sort of girl I would have foreseen you choosing as your wife."

"Those are your objections to her?" Darcy said. "She is not rich, has no noble relations—"

"Lady Catherine says her people are in trade," Bramwell interjected.

Slowly, Darcy nodded. "Her father is a gentleman, but her mother is from trade. However, I have met Mrs Bennet's younger brother and his wife, and you could not find a more respectable, kind couple." Turning to Fitzwilliam again, he added, "You are wrong, obviously, about the sort of lady I find suitable to be my wife. I could select someone matching what you said—and what your parents expect me, all three of us, to consider of utmost importance. Anne is sitting nearby, and from what her mother says, she would accept me. I might even find a modicum of contentment, especially if I believed it would have pleased my parents. But I want more," he added with fervour, his hands in loose fists. "I want to be happy. I want to look at my wife and thank God for sending her to me. I want to look forward to spending time with her, to enjoy her company, to know that I truly matter to her."

"You are in the enviable position of being able to make such a match." Fitzwilliam's voice was a touch wistful.

"And I shall exercise it," Darcy insisted.

"As well you should," Bramwell said. "I, for one, will support you. Just as I know you would support me if I decided to make an...unconventional choice of bride."

Darcy regarded him, his eyes narrowed. "Who is this latest lady love of yours?"

Fitzwilliam laughed. "Let us deal with your situation first. There will be time enough to upset our relations regarding his daring decision."

Darcy's gaze moved between the brothers as he once again asked, "Who?"

"You might be surprised, but, if she is foolish enough to succumb to him, she will make him an excellent wife and help him become the best man he could possibly be. Make a damn fine countess too, I reckon," Fitzwilliam assured him. "As for Elizabeth Bennet, I *do* like her. That must have been evident last spring in Kent. Certainly, you have known her long enough that no one could accuse you of acting on impulse or simply desire, and I can honestly tell them that nothing I saw in her suggests she is false and would trick you into marriage or accept you simply because you are rich. If she says she returns your feelings, then she does."

After regarding his cousins for a moment longer, Darcy nodded his thanks and then continued to walk. He required a period of exercise before returning to continue the battle with his family. *I must send them on their way as quickly as possible. Then I shall go to Elizabeth so that we can resume our conversation and finally reach an agreement!*

CHAPTER FOUR

Returning to the drawing room, Darcy was disappointed—but not surprised—to find his relations had remained where they had been when he, Bramwell, and Fitzwilliam had left them. There were cups and plates scattered on various tables, showing that one of Bingley's servants had supplied them with tea; it was more than they deserved. He yearned for a period of quiet reflection, but he knew that was currently impossible.

Before anyone else spoke, he did, his tone firm. "I am not, and never will be, engaged to Anne. Repeatedly saying that it is so does not make it true. I am not obligated by law to marry my cousin. Neither am I bound by honour—"

"You always led Anne and me to believe you agreed to the match," Lady Catherine interjected.

"I have not. What I have done is inform you time and again that I would *not* marry her."

"What of the discussions you had about marrying this autumn, last spring when you were in Kent?" Lord Romsley said, his question drowned by Lady Catherine's next statement.

"You only said you were not thinking of marriage or not ready for it yet," his aunt retorted. "Now that Georgiana is finished school, she needs a sister, as I told you at Easter."

"And I intend to give her an excellent one. No lady could be better suited to the role than Elizabeth Bennet!" Darcy said, struggling not to raise his voice.

As she had earlier, Lady Catherine spoke of his father making preparations for a marriage between Anne and Darcy. "All that was lacking was another month to see the business concluded. The contract would have been finalised."

"What year do you think it is? You cannot force me into a marriage, contract or not! There is no clergy in the world that would perform the ceremony against my wishes. It is 1812, not 1712, and people can no longer force their children to marry whomever they decide upon when they are in their cradles."

"Too true," Fitzwilliam said, barely loud enough to be heard.

Lady Catherine acted as though she had not, saying, "Perhaps not, but are you going to deny your parents' dearest wish for your future?"

"You know your father dreamt of uniting the two estates," Lord Romsley added. "It would create a further tie between his beloved wife's family and his own, as well as providing better for the tenants of both estates and future generations."

"Why are you so insistent on this matter?" Darcy asked him, managing to sound respectful. He truly did not understand it and supposed that, if he did, he would be able to overcome his uncle's objections.

The earl regarded him steadily. "I am attempting to protect our family, especially you, from allowing your emotions to cloud your judgment, emotions that most likely are fleeting."

Lady Catherine said, "I vow to you, Nephew, if you persist with this madness, I shall ensure everyone sees Elizabeth Bennet for what she is: a scheming minx who entrapped you with her base tricks and artfulness." Her features twisted into an almost menacing expression, though Darcy thought that might be more his imagination than reality. "I can ruin your reputation, ensure everyone knows you went against your parents' wishes and those of your family, that you have thrown over every expectation your cousin and I have, for a girl of inferior birth, one who does not even have a fortune to excuse your attraction. You will be castigated for breaking Anne's heart and for being a fool."

The heat in his belly was momentarily replaced by chilling dread. He did not fear for himself, but Elizabeth was another matter.

"Your father wanted it, and you would have obeyed him," Lord Romsley said. "You are to follow his instructions, even though he is no longer here to insist upon it himself."

"Because of a few letters he may have written years ago, without my knowledge, without even speaking to me of it or asking what *I* wanted? You cannot possibly believe that constitutes a legal basis for forcing me to—" Darcy cried.

"I say it is," the earl was quick to reply. "And if you choose to challenge it, I shall use my influence—"

"If you continue to threaten me, as I assume you intend to, our connexion will be at an end, sir." Darcy spoke with icy severity. He had had enough and was prepared to demand all six interlopers remove themselves from Netherfield at once. It was not his house, however, and he wondered where Bingley was; his friend might tell them to go, especially once he realised they were insulting the Bennets.

The countess made a noise of distress, and the earl held up his hands, palms facing Darcy, and, in a somewhat conciliatory manner, said, "Let us keep our tempers under good regulation." Looking towards his sister, she added, "*All* of us."

Darcy nodded and took in the other members of his family. Lady Romsley sat beside Anne, one hand resting on her niece's, while Bramwell and Fitzwilliam stood together near the fireplace once again. They met his eye, and he saw support in their expressions, for which he was grateful.

After a moment, the earl said, "Nephew, the simple fact is that your family expects your union to Anne, and you have implied for years that you would fulfil our expectations. Your continued stubbornness is ungentlemanly, and it is upsetting your aunt and cousin. It is too late to change your mind, just because some country miss has caught your eye." His voice was not unkind—more like that of a firm rather than angry parent.

Lady Catherine's tone had lost none of its bitter fury, however. She took a step towards him as she spoke. "That is the truth I shall advertise. There might not be a signed contract, but you *did* agree to marry Anne."

Darcy stared at his aunt for a long moment, the small threads of respect he had once had for her breaking one by one. Rather than direct his next comment to her, he turned to his cousin and asked, "Did I ever propose to you? Did I ever speak of our marriage, of you being my wife or living at Pemberley?"

Anne regarded him, unblinking. Her eyes were over-large in her thin face, and in them, he saw confusion. She did not respond; rather, her mother answered for her, as was her custom.

"Your engagement has never been a formal one, but that is immaterial."

"A fictional engagement," Bramwell said. "I understand they are quite *en vogue* this year."

Predictably, Fitzwilliam laughed, and the earl and countess reprimanded them. Darcy appreciated his effort to alleviate the tense atmosphere.

"Your father would be disappointed by you," Lord Romsley said to Darcy. "As would your mother, God rest her soul. I cannot believe you would choose to marry a girl who would bring nothing to your marriage, knowing it would make them unhappy and that, if your father were alive, he would never approve, never accept her as his daughter-in-law."

Darcy swallowed heavily, thinking his uncle's words were cruel and preyed on his grief. He hated the thought of displeasing his parents, whom he had loved and respected—but he believed the earl was wrong. "If my mother and father were alive and they met Elizabeth, they *would* welcome her to our family and understand exactly why she is the best lady to be my wife."

"There are benefits beyond, you know, fortune and connexions our future wives, whoever they might be, will bring to our marriages," Bramwell said, sounding unusually tentative. "Companionship and love."

Lady Catherine scoffed. "Love? You are going to decide who you like based on how pretty she is, how charming she looks when she flutters her eyelashes at you, how she stirs your—"

"Enough, Catherine," the earl hissed.

"Nephew," Lady Romsley said, drawing Darcy's attention. "You care for Anne already, and more can grow from such a beginning. Even if you never feel a grand passion such as novelists write about—and I doubt few ever do—there are different types of love, and you and she will share a good sort of steady, companionable love."

Lord Romsley said, "Anne, did you believe yourself bound to Darcy and that he agreed?" Anne nodded. "Is it what you want?" Again, his cousin nodded and dabbed at her eyes with her fine linen handkerchief.

The earl's next comment was directed at Darcy. "That ends the matter. Catherine and Anne, to say nothing of my wife and I—and I dare say Georgiana and your father's people—all anticipate the match. We shall all rejoice at your union, and you will be pleased to know how glad your parents would have been. It will bring prosperity and stability to your family for decades to come. Even were all this not true, you cannot possibly marry Miss Elizabeth Bennet. Who is her mother? Who are her aunts and uncles?"

"And her sister lately married that Wickham boy! No matter how her father and uncle tried to patch it up, I have been told by a reliable source that the couple eloped. Eloped!" Lady Catherine added, glee in her tone. "Darcy, you would tie yourself to your father's steward's son? The connexion would be shameful. There is nothing more to be said. You and Bramwell are both old enough to be married and produce heirs. You have responsibilities to this family. You will marry Anne, Bramwell will marry Lady Cassandra Nort—"

"I will not!" Bramwell interjected, his cheeks darkening.

Darcy scratched his forehead and spent the next moment listening to his eldest cousin and uncle debate the matter of Lady Cassandra Northcote. The truth was, the lady and Bramwell despised each other—possibly because they knew their parents wished for their marriage, possibly because they were just two exceedingly different people—but it was an eligible match that would strengthen certain political alliances.

"I do not like her," Bramwell said, carefully enunciating each word.

"What does that have to do with it?" Lady Catherine said, evidently unable to stop herself from taking part in a conversation that had nothing to do with her, to Darcy's way of thinking.

To Lady Romsley, Fitzwilliam said, "Would you really want your son to marry a lady he did not even like? And I assure you, he does not, and she certainly does not care for him."

"Well, no," the countess replied. "Not when you put it that way, but he and Lady Cassandra could learn to like each other."

With a loud bark of laughter, Bramwell said, "No, we could not."

"If not her, who will you marry?" she asked. "You are thirty years old, and it is past time for you to establish your own family."

"Tell them," Fitzwilliam advised his brother.

Briefly, Bramwell glared at him, then said, "Fine." He took a deep breath before admitting, "I intend to marry Miss Rebecca Darcy."

The silence that followed this statement was absolute. For himself, Darcy had not known of the viscount's interest in his cousin Rebecca, who was the daughter of his father's younger brother. While it was a relief to have the attention removed from his situation, with each passing minute, he was growing increasingly frustrated that his family was arguing in a home that did not belong to any of them. He said as much, calling it, "beyond comprehension that you are here, causing this scene in my friend's house."

Bramwell and Fitzwilliam were quick to agree.

"Nothing will be gained by continuing the discussion," Darcy went on. When his uncle interrupted, he sighed heavily, not bothering to hide his fatigue and vexation.

"While I do not agree that we are done with the discussion, I do agree it is enough for the moment. Let us all take some time to compose ourselves, consider everything that has been said"—he looked at Darcy as though telling him he needed to think about the excellent points he and Lady Catherine had made—"and we will resume it when we can do so rationally."

To himself, Darcy scoffed. He was resolved that it would not. With a curt nod at his uncle, a somewhat less stiff one to the countess—and none at all for his other aunt or Anne—he turned his back to his relations and walked towards the door, silently vowing that he would immediately write to his solicitor for whatever advice he could offer. He heard his uncle say, "As for you, Bramwell," just as he closed the door behind him.

Darcy sought sanctuary in his apartment and avoided his family as much as possible for the remainder of the day, even refusing to dine with them once he received word that Bingley would take the evening meal with the Bennets. How he envied his friend! What he would give for five minutes alone with Elizabeth. *But I must settle this matter with my family first! She has every right to want reassurance that they will not cause problems for us.* How could he ask her to trust him until he could give her that much at least?

The notion that he had a legal requirement to marry Anne was one he dismissed out of hand. Not even Lord Romsley could alter that reality. Even had his father and Lady Catherine agreed to a contract, Darcy himself had not signed it. The question of his honour being engaged was trickier, and one he would spend more time thinking about when he was less agitated. But no matter what his parents might have said in support of the union—and Darcy had only other people's assurances that it was what they wanted—he had always been against the scheme, a fact he had not kept secret. Whether he had been believed was another matter.

The true threat lay in what Lady Catherine and Lord Romsley would do, possibly with Lady Romsley's assistance. Would they make it known that the family had anticipated the marriage and they felt Darcy was failing to live up to his responsibilities, that, in short, he was going back on promises he had made?

In truth, if anything could have convinced him to marry Anne, it was knowing that it was what his father wanted. His mother's desires were also important to him, but for whatever reason, it had always been his father's approval he sought, possibly because Darcy had always thought of him as the best man he knew, and he wanted to be like him. Pleasing his relations by marrying Anne might also once have been enough to encourage Darcy to take such a step—but that had been before he had met Elizabeth.

"No one who knows Elizabeth would think me a fool for marrying her," he murmured. Within half a year of their marriage, the earl and countess and his other connexions—apart from Lady Catherine and Anne, he assumed—would understand why Elizabeth made the best possible wife for him. With her, he would be happy in a manner he had never believed possible, and she would be an exemplary helpmate, meaning those about him, from his sister to his tenants, would likewise benefit.

Lord and Lady Romsley must see that Lady Catherine was going too far, that she was allowing her apparent obsession with him marrying Anne to consume her. Darcy would have to discover what she had told them to convince them to invade Bingley's home as they had. It was especially galling because his three older relations hardly recognised his friend, thus compounding their rudeness.

The only members of his family Darcy spoke to again that day were Bramwell and Fitzwilliam; they came to his chamber late that evening, demanding entrance.

"I suppose I ought to thank you for adding your... what should I call it? Astonishing news?" he said to Bramwell. "You and Rebecca? Truly?"

"That is how you express your gratitude? Disbelief and mockery?" the viscount replied.

His cousins told him of the conversation at dinner—which apparently had been stilted and largely occupied with Lady Catherine reiterating that Darcy *had* promised himself to Anne and all the reasons he could not be permitted to marry Elizabeth.

"As though she has the right to permit or forbid you to do anything." Fitzwilliam laughed at the notion, but there was an obvious edge to it. Lady Catherine did not care whether or not she should do something; if it served her purposes, she proceeded, often displaying an unseemly lack of both respect and rationality. What did it matter if she was cruel and caused misery if she got her way in the end?

"How have you spent the past hours?" Fitzwilliam asked.

Darcy shrugged. "I attempted to write letters, but was unsuccessful." Reading through one he had intended to send to his solicitor, he found it was incomprehensible, which was a mark of the depths of his agitation. "I shall attend to it in the morning. I do not suppose your parents and our aunt have decided to depart? And Anne with them naturally." He often forgot about Anne, which should make him feel wretched. Instead, it exemplified why they would make such a terrible married couple.

Bramwell laughed, and Fitzwilliam rubbed the back of his neck as he shook his head.

"The dragon claims she will not go until you are prepared to attend her and Anne to Rosings where you will remain until your nuptials," Bramwell said, using his nickname for her. "She has finally given into madness, has she not?"

Darcy paced about the room, running his hands

through his hair. He would have to talk to them again, at least to convince them to leave Bingley's home. Saying as much to his cousins, he added, "But I am determined never to go to Rosings again. Lady Catherine has gone too far this time. The way she spoke to Elizabeth, the horrible names she called her, are unforgivable, let alone her interference in my affairs. Tomorrow morning. There is no need for you two to be here. If you do not wish to return to London—which is what I think you should do—explore the neighbourhood. Go to Meryton. It is pretty enough, and the bookseller is quite decent."

In the end, the three of them agreed that Bramwell and Fitzwilliam would leave Darcy to talk to the earl, countess, and Lady Catherine alone, but they would not, as Bramwell said, 'abandon you to the fools' by returning to town.

CHAPTER FIVE

It was a largely sleepless night for Darcy until exhaustion overcame him in the early hours, permitting him two or three hours of rest. As soon as his valet, Quinn, was aware that he had wakened, he said that the earl's man had delivered a message. Lord Romsley wanted to see him before breakfast; Darcy was to go to his bedchamber. The vessels in his head immediately began to throb. The note from his uncle was enough to make Darcy long to hide under the bedcovers and avoid the day, which he anticipated would be filled with frustrating, enraging, and repetitive disputes regarding his choices in life.

After consulting the mantel clock, he said, "I shall write a response to be delivered to his lordship in half an hour. Should anyone enquire, I am not yet awake."

Sometime later, dressed and with a much-needed cup of strong tea warming his belly, Darcy went in search of

Bingley. The note to his uncle had claimed there would be no time to meet before the breakfast hour. In reality, he simply wanted to delay speaking to him—or Lady Catherine, or even the countess. He needed more sustenance before he could listen to their entreaties—demands—that he give up Elizabeth and accept the so-called rightness of a union with Anne.

At least at breakfast, I can count on Fitzwilliam and Bramwell's support. His cousins would also provide distraction.

He found Bingley sitting alone in the drawing room. His friend gave him a look of sympathy, and, with a sigh, Darcy took a chair across from him.

"So?" Bingley asked. They had not spoken since he had departed to Longbourn with Elizabeth and Miss Bennet the previous day; by the time he had returned, Darcy had retired to his chamber.

Darcy sighed again and shook his head. "It was not pleasant. No doubt, you heard enough to understand why they have come. I cannot apologise enough for my family's intrusion. It is unconscionably rude of them."

Bingley waved this away. "You had no way of knowing they would follow you to Hertfordshire, nor have you control over their behaviour." He blushed. "Now it is I who must apologise. I should not speak so of them."

Darcy gave a low, humourless laugh. "After what you witnessed, after how horribly they spoke of Elizabeth, they deserve far worse. They will not succeed."

Scratching his jaw and chuckling, Bingley admitted

that he had not been aware of Darcy's interest in Elizabeth. "She said little yesterday, even to Jane and me. Understandably, I suppose. I mean, she would not wish to speak of it to her parents or sisters."

"How is she?" Darcy heard the slight tremble in his voice. Above anything, he wanted to see Elizabeth, to hold her in his arms and promise her that all was well. That would not be true, however, until he managed to send his family away with the promise that they would no longer interfere in his business.

Bingley contorted his features into several expressions, none of which Darcy could entirely interpret. "Well...she was rather quiet, which is unusual for her. As I am sure you know. I could not say exactly what she felt, but if I had to guess, I would say she was as shocked by what happened, as we all were, and anxious on your behalf."

He suppressed a desire to sigh, feeling he had done quite enough of it already. "I would like nothing more than to say I shall go to see her at once or as soon as the hour is reasonable, but..." Bingley nodded his understanding. "Already, my uncle requested a private discussion. My hope for today is that I shall convince them to leave, ideally before noon."

Bingley nodded again, this time vigorously. "Jane suggested I join the Bennets for breakfast, and I think I shall. I would not have wanted to leave without talking to you first, but I imagine my presence will not make the situation easier. Naturally, your relations would wish to speak to you alone."

Darcy agreed and promised that he would join him at Longbourn once his family were gone, supposing the hour was not too late.

Breakfast went as Darcy had anticipated it would; the atmosphere was both frosty and heated, with more than himself feeling agitated and angry, from what he could tell from the expressions and voices they all used—apart from Anne, who remained silent. Afterwards, he had yet another long discussion with the earl and Lady Catherine that left him wanting to hit his head against a wall. Bramwell had joked about their aunt going mad, but it was Darcy who felt that he was. The cause was the endless circle of arguments he felt trapped in, back and forth and back and forth they went, neither side willing to accept anything the other said.

Nothing was resolved, although to Darcy's surprise, the earl appeared to want to find a compromise of some sort. What that might be under the circumstances, Darcy did not know, and it seemed his uncle did not either. Lady Catherine refused to settle for anything other than Darcy's immediate removal to Kent and vow to remain at Rosings until after he was wed to Anne.

Darcy was also subject to a conversation with Lady Romsley. The countess was gentler in her statements; she did not demand, but she spoke at some length of why it would be 'so much better and easier' for him to marry a lady from their own circle. "If not Anne, then another.

There are many eligible girls who would be a credit to your name and who would make excellent mistresses for Pemberley, to say nothing of sisters for Georgiana."

"Anne is hardly of our circle," Darcy retorted. "When was the last time she was in town? How many balls and soirées has she attended? I recall one occasion at which she was at the opera, and it proved too much for her. Or so Lady Catherine said. We all know Anne would not have told us."

"I understand you are displeased by having us question your decisions, Nephew, but you need not use such a belligerent tone with me."

Darcy's cheeks warmed at the reprimand. "I apologise, Lady Romsley. You are correct, and I regret my words. I find the present situation...displeasing."

"But you must understand our concern. I am well aware that my sister-in-law's manner can be strident. Unyielding. But Catherine and Anne have long anticipated you would fulfil your parents' hopes. Catherine told us you spoke of having the wedding soon when you were at Rosings in the spring."

Before she could say more, he held up a hand, palm towards her. "With respect, I have heard enough of what my father and mother supposedly desired for my future, to say nothing of my aunt and cousin. I can only insist, as clearly as possible, that nothing will change my opinion on the matter. As to her and I discussing a wedding, I assure you, I did *not* participate in such a conversation." It was possible Lady Catherine had blathered about it, but she had often spoken thus, regardless of his assertions of disinterest, thus he paid no attention. "As for your suggestion that I find another lady from the *ton*, please recall that, despite the numerous parties and so forth I have attended—in town and elsewhere—I have never met a lady I wanted to marry, that I felt I could be happy with. Until I met Miss Elizabeth. I understand my choice might surprise you, but I am convinced she and she alone will suit me, and I have felt this way for many months."

Lady Romsley regarded him. The way her head was tilted to the side and the gentle crease between her eyebrows gave the impression that she was sad and perhaps resigned. "If you are truly so set against marrying Anne, then I shall not try to change your mind. I do not know why my sister-in-law is convinced you agreed to wed this autumn when you say you did not, but that is immaterial, in my opinion. Of much greater import is this girl you wish to marry. You owe it to yourself, your estate, and the memory of your parents to make a more prudent match."

"I owe it to myself to make a marriage that will ensure my happiness," he countered. "Trust me enough to know that I would not marry a lady who was incapable of being a good sister and mistress."

It took about ten minutes longer before he could escape the countess, and Darcy was unsure what she presently thought regarding the circumstances. Bramwell and Fitzwilliam were nearby and wanted to go to a quiet room so that he could tell them about the recent conversations, but he put them off.

"I have letters to write, and I do not want to delay sending them," he insisted. "See if you can convince your parents to return to town. I think they are willing, but they will not go unless Lady Catherine does, and she insists she will not unless I agree to go with her and Anne."

"We shall do our best," Fitzwilliam promised. "After that, my brother and I shall follow your suggestion from last night and go into Meryton for a while."

To no great surprise, Mr Bingley was at Longbourn in time for breakfast. He gave Elizabeth an awkward smile, but otherwise, he said nothing to her of what she most wanted to hear, meaning that Mr Darcy would be there soon and that his family had all returned to town or Kent or wherever they had come from. But it would not be so simple to resolve the situation with them; Lady Catherine, if not the earl and countess, would not be easily convinced to support his desire to marry Elizabeth.

I wonder if, hearing their objections, he will change his mind. The notion worried her, but only briefly. Lady Catherine had voiced her opinion of the match to him after visiting her at Longbourn, and that had not stopped him from returning. Elizabeth did not suppose she would soon forget his first proposal, although she had laughingly told herself she was resolved to do just that upon the first anniversary of their wedding. At present, she discovered it left her feeling uncertain—not so much in him but in the likelihood that they could have a happy future together, although she was not certain why. It might only be because it seemed that so much had happened over the last two months. Starting from meeting Mr Darcy again in Derbyshire, which had awakened something in her she had not known was possible. Then, there was all the anxiety of Lydia's elopement and eventual marriage, and she could not forget how irritated she had been during the Wickhams' stay in Hertfordshire! Those days had felt long indeed. Mr Darcy's earlier return when he had been silent and watchful had confused her and robbed her of sleep. Currently, Mr Bingley's unwillingness to look at her, let alone say more than was demanded by politeness, only made her discomfiture worse.

After eating, a scheme was devised to walk into Meryton, the day being fair. The gentleman displayed his usual willingness to escort Elizabeth and her sisters, and as Mrs Bennet made no objections, they soon set out. Mary attempted to speak to her, but soon gave up, accusing her of being, 'too dull today'. She asked if Elizabeth had a headache, and when she said no, said, "Then I shall leave you to your thoughts."

Thereafter, Mary chatted with Kitty, while Jane and Mr Bingley were lost in themselves, as usual. For her own part, Elizabeth attempted to distract herself by taking in the changes brought about by the autumn weather and making a note that Kitty's coat was growing thin near the hem and would need replacing before long.

Not long after entering the market town, Kitty made a

noise of surprise and said, "Who could they be? They must be guests at Haye-Park, do you not think? But Miss Goulding—"

"They are Mr Darcy's cousins," Elizabeth interjected, her voice flat. She had seen them at once, and it was obvious whom her sister meant. While strangers were not uncommon in Meryton, by their clothing alone, it was obvious that the viscount and colonel were significant persons, and that was unusual.

"Mr Darcy's cousins?" Kitty said. "Are they staying at Netherfield? When did they arrive? How did you know who they were?"

"You might try asking one question at a time," she said, knowing she sounded as peevish as she felt.

Fortunately, Mr Bingley chose to respond. He gave an embarrassed sounding laugh and glanced at Elizabeth before saying, "They came yesterday. Did I forget to mention it? How stupid of me. I do not think they will be here long. Shall we go to Mr Miller's?" The man's shop sold a wide variety of sundries and was a favourite amongst the Bennets.

"Are you not going to introduce us?" Kitty said. Even without looking at her, Elizabeth knew her sister was eager to meet the gentlemen, which was understandable. There was little new to occupy them in the neighbourhood of late, apart from Jane's engagement.

"Oh, um, yes, of course," Mr Bingley replied.

Despite preferring to overlook their presence, Elizabeth could not miss that the brothers were walking towards their party; there would be no escaping speaking to them. *Perhaps I should not wish it*, she reflected. They might have a message from Mr Darcy. It would have made more sense for Mr Bingley to deliver it, but she did not care who told her what was happening at Netherfield presently; she just wanted—*needed*—to know. And she had liked Colonel Fitzwilliam when they had met in the spring. It was possible he would be pleased to have his cousin marry her, even if no one else in the family would be. Miss Darcy, too, had been friendly. But had she known that her brother had a romantic interest in Elizabeth? And, given the girl's own past with Mr Wickham, would she object to Mr Darcy being connected to the despicable man through marriage?

Stop, Lizzy! she reprimanded, surreptitiously pinching herself. This sort of gloomy thinking was unlike her. Then again, she reflected, there had been occasions when her thoughts were particularly displeasing, including her earlier sentiments regarding Mr Darcy and his behaviour. But that had been before she loved him, before her dearest wish was to become his wife.

Mr Bingley made the necessary introductions, adding, "The walk from Longbourn is pleasant, and it is an amusing way to pass the time."

"Darcy recommended we come," Colonel Fitzwilliam explained. "He thought we might like to get out of the house for a while."

"And so we did," the viscount said. "You will not mind if we join you?"

Jane assured them they were welcome to do so, and they continued on their way. Kitty managed to capture the gentlemen's attention for a few minutes, but when they reached the first shop they intended to visit, a change occurred that saw everyone apart from Elizabeth and the brothers enter. She remained with them when it was apparent from the looks Colonel Fitzwilliam was giving her that they wished to talk to her.

"It must have been a terrible surprise to see our family gathered at Netherfield," the colonel said, keeping his voice low so that their conversation remained as private as possible. "Distressing, even, I might say, given what was said by some of the party. I trust you have not suffered excessively. I know it would reassure my cousin if I could tell him as much."

Elizabeth gave him a brief, not entirely sincere smile, but said nothing.

"We had no notion what my aunt intended, only that she was displeased with something Darcy was about to do," Lord Bramwell explained. "I claim curiosity as my excuse for insisting I accompany my parents, aunt, and cousin Anne, though my brother would likely say he felt it was his duty to protect Darcy. His military training, you see?" There was a mischievous twinkle in his eyes that made Elizabeth think she might like him if the circumstances were different.

"Knowing Lady Catherine, I believed...saner voices might be needed," the colonel said. "You have spent enough time in her company to understand what I mean."

"Are you implying that you have not come to tell Mr Darcy that you do not approve of his interest in me, unlike your relations? Or is your intention only to offer… less strident arguments against his choice?" Elizabeth asked. She took in the busy street, hoping to escape the notice of the worst gossips in her social circle. If her mother learnt that she had stood outside the shop, speaking to two such eligible men, she would insist on knowing every word they had spoken.

Lord Bramwell laughed. "Very good, Miss Elizabeth, very good indeed. You have convinced me. Darcy *must* marry you."

Her brow furrowed, Elizabeth regarded him. It seemed an odd response to her questions.

The colonel rolled his eyes. "There is a lady Bramwell is interested in marrying. Our parents, to say nothing of our aunt, are not overly fond of the potential match, which they only learnt of yesterday. His situation is not unlike yours and Darcy's. Our parents have chosen another lady for him and consider the one he prefers…"

"Inferior?" Elizabeth suggested when he did not go on. "Not worthy of his position in life? Would she bring disgrace to his name?"

"What they think and what is true are worlds apart," the viscount said, his voice holding none of the humour it had earlier. "You might find this particularly amusing, and I only mention it since everyone else in the family now knows. The lady is Darcy's paternal cousin, the daughter of his father's younger brother. A Darcy is not good enough? Ha!"

After studying his brother for a long moment, the colonel turned again to Elizabeth. "The issue, according to our parents, is that she is not titled, her fortune, while respectable, is considerably less than that of the lady they want him to marry, and my father would not strengthen his relationship with a political ally. My aunt's arguments against the union are...somewhat less rational."

"There is no rational objection to Rebecca Darcy," the viscount hissed.

Colonel Fitzwilliam held up his hands in a placating manner. "I agree. I would be very pleased to have her as a sister-in-law."

Elizabeth sighed. She had no patience for the conversation. Another time, she might find it diverting, but her thoughts and concerns were entirely directed at Mr Darcy currently. "You suppose if you support Mr Darcy's decision to overlook your relations' wishes and marry where he likes...?"

"He will do the same for me," the viscount said with a nod. "I am sure you will see my cousin soon. He was much occupied this morning—writing letters and attempting to evade my aunt. I do not expect she would allow him to escape the house easily, in any case, knowing as she does that he would find the company at Longbourn far more agreeable. But look for him tomorrow morning. I am devising a means to secure him a period of freedom. Fitzwilliam will help, and I shall even convince my mother that Darcy must be allowed to talk to you. She is the most reasonable of them, and my hopes—for both myself, and you and Darcy—lie primarily with her."

The colonel agreed, and Elizabeth quietly thanked

them. Mary joined them, followed soon after by the remainder of their party, and they continued to pass a short interval together before the two gentlemen returned to Netherfield and Mr Bingley and Jane led the way back to Longbourn.

CHAPTER SIX

After leaving his cousins, who he understood intended to follow his advice and visit the market town, Darcy returned to his apartment. He allowed himself a moment to imagine Bramwell and Fitzwilliam encountering Elizabeth during their excursion—given she and her sisters liked to walk into Meryton. They would inform her that they did not agree with their parents' and Lady Catherine's arguments, and, later, they could tell him how she looked, if she was well. One of his greatest fears at present was that she would decide to give up on him. Why would she anticipate making such people her family, knowing they would despise her, possibly seek to turn other people against her so that she would be left friendless, with her family shamed?

The only thing for him to do was to prove to her that there was no truth to the notion that his father had been intent on the match between his son and niece, certainly not to the extent Lady Catherine insisted, and—what might be even more valuable—find a way to convince the earl and countess to cease their objections. Similarly, he must assure her that his other close connexions—his uncle Darcy and his family—would welcome her.

Unlike the previous day, Darcy was able to write a coherent letter to his solicitor asking that he determine whether his father had ever made arrangements for him to marry Anne beyond the letters Lady Catherine claimed to have exchanged with him. Darcy doubted that he had, given his unexpected death and the fact they had never spoken of it. Still, demonstrating that would support his side of their dispute. Next, he wrote to Georgiana and Mrs Annesley. After Lady Catherine's visit to him in London, during which she had told him of coming to Hertfordshire and confronting Elizabeth, he had told his sister and her companion that they should prepare to travel to town. Mr Potter, Pemberley's steward, would accompany them on the journey, ensuring their safety and comfort; his sister lived near London, and he would be glad for the opportunity to see her.

What Darcy had not informed Georgiana of was that he would soon be proposing to Elizabeth. Either she would accept, in which case he would like his sister there to join in his happiness, or she would again refuse him, and he would require his sister's company to ease his sorrow. He did not believe the latter would happen, but if it did, he would take Georgiana on a holiday, seek diversion to overcome what would be the end of his hopes regarding the only lady he could possibly give his heart to. He wrote:

Stay at Pemberley for now. I do not wish to explain the reasons more than to say Lady Catherine is not behaving as she ought. She is attempting to bully me, and I do not want you to be dragged into the disgusting situation, which I am working to resolve. She would seek to worry and browbeat you until you agreed with her. Do not worry, my dear sister. I shall explain it all to you when we are together, and I do not imagine this will result in more than a slight delay. Possibly, you will receive a letter from me the day after this one arrives telling you to have your bags packed.

No sooner had he finished the letter than Fitzwilliam joined him. They sat in matching leather wing chairs by the fireplace.

"The earl insisted on having yet another conversation with my brother about your cousin Rebecca," the colonel explained. "I think it would be an excellent match for Bramwell. She would only accept him if she felt true affection for him—if she loved him—and she is outspoken enough to demand he behave as an adult. In short, that he be more serious." He made a noise that suggested sudden realisation. "What I have been thinking is that she complements him well. What he lacks, she can provide, including knowing he is valued for who he is and not just his position in life, and what she lacks, he can provide."

"What do you imagine my cousin needs from him?" Darcy was curious, but he asked more because it seemed Fitzwilliam expected it.

"Perhaps nothing she feels is all that important to her life, but he is rich and will be an earl. And you know he would be a loyal and fiercely protective husband to a woman he truly loves." Darcy nodded, and Fitzwilliam continued. "I realised that you have also chosen a lady that complements you well."

Darcy arched his brow, silently encouraging his cousin to continue.

"She is lively, and you need someone who will encourage you to be less serious. She is also intelligent, which you require in a lady, because you would be bored and annoyed with a wife who was neither. And she would gain from your position in life. From what she told me last spring, her education was...informal, and I suspect she would value what you could tell and show her of the world." Fitzwilliam smiled broadly. "I congratulate you, Darcy. You have made an excellent decision, not only for yourself, but also for Georgiana. I can see that Miss Elizabeth would be just the sister she needs."

"Now if only you could convince your parents," Darcy said, his tone dry. "Since you have said nothing of it, I assume they have not agreed to depart?"

Fitzwilliam shook his head. "Bramwell and I have only now returned from Meryton. We saw Miss Elizabeth there, with Bingley and her sisters."

"And?" Darcy asked, leaning forwards in his eagerness to hear more of the encounter.

"We spoke to her alone for a few minutes, really just long enough to assure her that my brother and I do not hold the same views as our parents and aunt, that we shall do what we can to alter Mother and Father's opinion, and, finally, that she should expect to see you tomorrow morning."

Darcy nodded and sat back. His gaze averted, he ran a hand over his mouth and contemplated being with Elizabeth the next day.

"When I came to find you, my mother was attempting to reason with Lady Catherine, but we both know that is a hopeless business," Fitzwilliam said.

"She must be desperate to see Anne married. Though it is not necessary, given her fortune." Darcy quietly chuckled. "Why do *you* not offer to marry her? Then we might all go about our lives and leave Bingley to enjoy his house."

Fitzwilliam reached across the distance between them and punched his arm. "She does not want a penniless colonel as a son-in-law."

"You are not penniless."

"I am comparatively poor and, most importantly, I do not have a grand estate or title that would make me good enough for her precious daughter, who, as we have been assured for years, deserves only the best," Fitzwilliam said sarcastically.

Darcy sniggered at the thought that Anne—insipid, in poor health, and generally devoid of attractions—could capture the attention of any gentleman who did not require her one redeeming quality: Rosings. "Admit it, even if you were mistaken or your father could convince Lady Catherine to accept a match between you, you would not want it. Anne as your wife?"

"It feels wrong to admit it, and I do pity our cousin and wish her life had been more agreeable, but no. If it were a matter of Anne having someone to ensure her a secure future, keep her safe, or what have you, and to oversee the estate, then I suppose I might. But if she sought a true husband, one who would treat her as a wife and who married her for affection? No. More to the point, I would never want Lady Catherine as a mother-in-law."

Darcy nodded to indicate he understood his cousin's sentiments. He supposed if there were no Elizabeth Bennet and several more years had passed without his meeting another lady he could foresee marrying, he might have considered his cousin, if only because his family favoured it and he would gain Rosings. But even under those circumstances, he doubted he would have done more than spend a moment debating it; the simple fact was that he did not care for Anne and would not want a closer connexion to his aunt. That was even more certain after her recent actions.

"What are you going to do?" Fitzwilliam asked.

Resting his head against the chair and closing his eyes, Darcy spoke of the questions he had posed to his lawyer and the letter he had written to Georgiana. "Other than that, I must speak to Elizabeth, to reassure her that your parents—if not Lady Catherine—will see reason. I might resort to threats of my own. If our aunt is willing to issue them, saying she will ruin me, then I shall not hesitate to return the favour. You will join me in again encouraging them to depart and leave me to make my own choices?"

Fitzwilliam nodded, and they spent the next while speaking of other matters before preparing for dinner.

Several hours after she returned from Meryton, Mr Bennet called Elizabeth into his book-room. He sat behind the old walnut desk from her, his fingers steepled and covering his mouth, and studied her for a long moment while she sat opposite him on a brocade armchair. For some reason, her heart began to beat more quickly the longer he remained silent. Likely it was because of the sense of unease that had settled over her since going to Netherfield with Mr Darcy and finding his family there. The earlier conversation with Viscount Bramwell and Colonel Fitzwilliam had done little to alleviate it.

If I had only seen him today, or if Mr Bingley had brought a message from him, then perhaps I would not feel as though something truly awful is about to befall me. It was similar to the sensation she had had the morning in Lambton when she had told Mr Darcy of Lydia's elopement. How certain she had then been that all association between them was at an end! Yet, he had returned to her and proposed for the second time, fulfilling a wish she had hardly been willing to admit she had.

Her father cleared his throat and lowered his hands, the fingers of one beginning to tap out an irregular rhythm on the wooden tabletop. "I have been hearing of the most extraordinary goings-on. A carriage purportedly belonging to my cousin Collins's patroness—the same Lady Catherine you were so fortunate as to be in company with last spring—has been seen at Netherfield Park. It appears that another, even more impressive equipage, was also spotted. It must belong to very wealthy people, and ones of some importance, given the crests upon the doors. Mr Darcy's relations, I assume?"

Swallowing the lump that had formed in her throat, Elizabeth said that he was correct, explaining, "His aunt, Lady Catherine, is there, along with her daughter. The other carriage belongs to his uncle, the Earl of Romsley. With him are his wife and their two sons." Her father's tone—at once sarcastic and deceptively calm—made her wary and increasingly sick with apprehension.

He made a noise of interest and slowly nodded before saying, "And why have they come? I know you saw them yesterday. I recall Mr Bingley's garbled tale this morning of a servant finding you whilst you and Jane were walking with the gentlemen to say that Mr Darcy was needed at Netherfield at once. I admit, I was surprised to see Mr Darcy here again so soon. Perhaps I ought to first ask what Lady Catherine wanted with you when she was here—when was it? Last week? The week before?"

Elizabeth was unsure how much to admit, feeling that her past with Mr Darcy was a secret between the two of them. One that was precious in its own way, because it had helped them both come to a better understanding of themselves and each other—she believed he would agree with her—and which would allow them to share the most marvellous love. The pause before she spoke was brief, but long enough that her father took note of it. His brow arched, and he kept a steady eye on her.

Well, there is nothing for it. I shall have to explain some part of my connexion to Mr Darcy. "I suppose I should first tell you that I met Mr Darcy again this past summer, when my aunt, uncle, and I were in Lambton, which is near his estate."

"You did? Was he as disagreeable as he was last autumn?" There was humour in his voice, and she was not sure whether he expected her to answer yes—in which case they might share a laugh—or no, in which case, he might find reason to tease her.

"He showed us exceptional friendliness and hospitality. We were to dine at Pemberley, and would have, had not I received Jane's letters that same day."

"That is surprising, especially regarding the Gardiners. What accounts for his remarkable change in manner, for such it must have been, compared to when we first knew him?"

A proposal and refusal I shall never tell you about. I can hardly believe he not only accepted my reproofs then, but acted on them. It is because he loves me. But did he love her enough to overcome the entreaties—insistence—of his relations to give her up? Try as she might to push aside the memory, she heard his words from Easter when he had spoken of the inferiority of her connexions and how his family would object to their marriage. He had been correct; she had evidence of it herself.

In answer to her father, she said, "I could hardly say,

but he was polite. You might not recall that we also met when I was in Kent."

"You did?" he interjected. "Ah, yes, I seem to recall you or Collins mentioning it. I did not have the impression you saw much of him."

Knowing she was prevaricating, Elizabeth said, "It was enough to show me he was more than the arrogant man we initially believed him to be. Much of the general poor impression of him was due to Mr Wickham's tales of mistreatment, but we know now that he lied."

Once again, he interrupted her. "Do we? My son-in-law is hardly an honourable man, but that does not mean he lied about Mr Darcy's actions."

"He did," she insisted, her voice heated. "You cannot truly doubt that, Papa, not after everything we have learnt of Mr Wickham!" Mr Bennet shrugged, and she quickly continued, hoping to avoid listening to him disparage the man she loved. "Then, this summer, we were able to meet as friends"—she tightly clasped her hands and continued in a rush—"and Mr Darcy wishes to marry me."

Her father's fingers stilled, and, although the sound of his drumming them on the desk had been faint, the resulting silence was heavy. At length, he said, "Mr Darcy wishes to marry you? And what are your feelings on the matter, Lizzy?"

The back of her neck burnt. "I return his affection. In fact, we were just about to settle the matter when Mr Bingley's servant found us."

Yet again, her father did not respond immediately.

When he did, his words were not ones to please her. In short order, he forced her to admit that there was more to her connexion to Mr Darcy than what she had told him, and, soon after, she found herself obliged to explain the whole of it—including their argument in Kent, Lady Catherine's true purpose in coming to Longbourn, and what had happened at Netherfield the previous day. To say he was displeased was an understatement, though she was not sure if it was so much by what had happened or that it had and he had been unaware of it all.

His sentiments were nothing to her own by the time he finally permitted her to leave the book-room and return to her chamber. She would not leave it again that day, too indisposed to join the family for dinner. She even refused to speak to Jane when her sister came to enquire into her well-being.

CHAPTER SEVEN

Early the next morning, Darcy set out for a walk, hoping that he would meet Elizabeth, despite the heavy clouds that threatened rain imminently. Fitzwilliam and Bramwell had lent their assistance by distracting their parents and Lady Catherine to ensure the trio remained unaware that he had slipped out of the house. He felt increasingly desperate to talk to her, even just to see her, knowing she alone could soothe his ever-simmering fury at his relations. He found her pacing in a small clearing on the stream-side path between Netherfield and Longbourn. At once, he stepped towards her, intending to embrace her; it was not a conscious decision, but given their shared love—which he did not doubt—it seemed both right and necessary.

To his surprise, she retreated, keeping the distance between them steady. A stab of disappointment and fear shot through him, and he almost raised a hand to his heart. The expression on her face was apprehensive, sorrowful even, though she was not as distressed as she had been in Lambton when she had learnt the news of her sister's elopement. Darcy shook his head, not knowing what to make of it. Surely she was as glad to see him as he was her, especially that they could speak privately! But, on reflection, she must be confused and concerned. With this in mind, he quickly greeted her and explained what was happening with his family. She periodically nodded as though she understood, and she asked many questions.

When he had finished his recitation, she said, "I appreciate how open you have been. Was Lady Catherine correct when she said that no one would accept our marriage? Accept me? Would Lord and Lady Romsley and your remaining family? Do you think your friends and acquaintances in town and in Derbyshire would? Please, do not hide the truth from me."

He longed to give her the reassurances that she evidently required, but he would not be dishonest with her, not even slightly; it would damage their relationship, and she was too wise not to see through any clever wording he used to avoid giving a response. Nevertheless, knowing it was not enough, he found himself saying, "I could hardly say how everyone will act."

"Your family, your nearest relations—those here presently and the others I have not met—how would they behave? Lord Bramwell would support our union for his own reasons, from what he told me yesterday, and Colonel Fitzwilliam claims he does too. What of Miss Darcy?"

"Georgiana was very glad to meet you."

"That does not mean she would like to have me as a sister," Elizabeth said before he could go on. She turned her chin away from him and kept her gaze on a group of bushes. "Perhaps it was too much to hope for, that, after everything—"

Panic tightened around his heart like an iron band, and his voice came out as a harsh gasp. "Elizabeth, no!"

"I do not want to feel this way," she said insistently. "To doubt that it would be in our best interests—yours and mine as individuals. I hate the notion of inserting myself into your family, of causing such strife, possibly ending with you estranged from people who are so important to you. I wish the situation were different, that there was no question of whether you were at liberty."

"I am." He spoke too loudly, but he felt as though he were being strangled and had to force the words out. She could not be telling him there was no hope; that was utterly, entirely unacceptable! There was no surer way to create a breach between him and his relations than to have their interference end with his Elizabeth sending him away forever.

Her eyes met his again. "Are you? Legally, I suppose you are, from what I understand of the law. And, in another sense, I believe you are, that you would not pursue me if you felt at all honour-bound to Miss de Bourgh. But there is more to this. Would you be happy if, in marrying me, your family disavowed you, even if the consequence was being always at odds with them? You cannot tell me it would not happen when, at this very moment—less than three miles away—are people who matter to you and who are telling you directly they hate the notion of you choosing me. You told me yourself last April that they would dislike it. I thought little of it, I suppose, not then and not of late, not even after Lady Catherine's call last month. I see now that I ought to have considered it. If the situation were reversed, if I knew accepting you would make my family so unhappy, that they would separate themselves from me…"

"You would not accept me," he said. Tears burned at the back of his eyes, but he refused to show his distress. Certain there was more she was not telling him, something that drove her to speak thus, she did not deserve to see how wretched he was at the thought of where this conversation was leading. Had one of his relations sought her out without him knowing it? Had Bramwell or Fitzwilliam said more to her than they had told him?

After a brief silence, she said, "There would be no easy path. I would be torn in two, hating the alternatives. To lose the very people who have been my world, who have loved me and accepted me, been the people I have laughed and cried with, who I know would always be there to support me when I needed it, to console or celebrate with me, or to lose the man I love, the only one I can imagine sharing my life with, being happy with."

Squeezing his hands into fist to hide how they trembled, he slowly shook his head. "What has happened? Has my uncle or one of my aunts done yet more to disgust you, to put these doubts into your heart? My cousins—"

"No. I am simply aware that I can spare you having to make a decision between me and your family." She paused and pressed her lips together; by the way she blinked rapidly, he knew she was as close to crying as he was. "I know how much you respect and value them, and I do not believe you would ever be truly happy if you lost your connexion to them, especially to your sister."

"Do you think I shall continue to respect and value them knowing they have cost me the only woman I have ever loved or wanted to marry?"

Tears had begun to fall down her cheeks, and she wiped them away with a gloved hand. "Perhaps part of me is afraid that those feelings would fade when you were forced to confront what marrying me cost you."

Again, he shook his head, this time more vigorously. "I do not believe you are saying this of your own volition. Please, Elizabeth, I beg you, let us not misunderstand or keep the truth from each other, not again."

She regarded him for a long moment, doing nothing to hide her distress, before nodding and telling him of a recent conversation with Mr Bennet. "I had no alternative but to explain our entire history. He would settle for nothing less."

With mounting horror, Darcy took in the situation. Mr Bennet had informed her that he would not grant his consent to their marriage, even should Darcy find a way out of his present dispute. While the older gentleman thought it was nonsensical that there could be a legal requirement for him to marry his cousin, there were considerations beyond the law.

"He said that we could not know whether honour required it of you," she said, hastily adding, "but you say there is not, and I believe you. What matters most to him, what made him tell me I must have this conversation with you—" She paused for a long moment to regain her composure; he stood silently, not wanting to do or say that which would make this more difficult for her. "My father has decided that he would not give his consent to our marriage, because he has no interest in angering people of Lord Romsley's position. We might live in this small out of the way place, but who knows what it might mean for our family, including the Gardiners and Jane. My father asked me to consider whether our situation might cause problems for her engagement and marriage and acceptance amongst Mr Bingley's circle. He is part of your social sphere in town, which means she will be too."

She took a deep breath before continuing. Her eyes, which had always so enraptured him, were on his, shining with tears, but also love and the strength he so admired in her. "Although I shall be one-and-twenty soon, the thought of marrying knowing he disapproves, knowing I would marry without his blessing..."

"You would hate it, as would I, because I understand how much you esteem him and would worry it would affect your connexion to your mother and sisters. I shall speak to him."

"You may try, but despite whatever impression you have of him being less involved in our lives than he should be, my father can be an incredibly stubborn man. That is especially true since this summer. I tried to change his mind, please believe that I did." He nodded, and she went on. "I hate to say it, but I do not think you will sway him, not at present. The only thing that might is if he were convinced that your family would welcome me and embrace our marriage."

His darling, beloved Elizabeth stepped towards him and held out a hand, which he grasped. She said, "Our connexion has hardly been conventional or easy. At first, we completely misunderstood each other. I never would have guessed we would be standing together like this. When we parted in Kent, I did not expect we would ever see each other again. Then we met at Pemberley, and, for a time, I was filled with hope and anticipated joy. It disappeared at our parting but then reappeared when you were here last month. I truly believed that, despite everything, we might have a chance at happiness together. And yet, here we are. How many times do we have to confront these obstacles before we admit—"

He would not listen to her say the words that would surely rip his heart into pieces. "I never saw you as a pessimistic person."

"I am not," she said, lightly pressing his hand. "I am angry and disappointed, and sad, tired and confused, and more as well. I do not know what to do! If I had some sense of purpose, if I could think of even one step I might take to make our situation how I want it to be, then I would. Can you think of anything?" There was a challenge in her tone, and he realised she was encouraging him—pleading with him—to do whatever necessary to find a way to convince her father and his relations.

"I am trying," he vowed softly. He took a small step closer to her and felt a tear slide down his cheek.

"I know," she whispered. "I pray you are successful, and I *will* do whatever I can. But if nothing changes, then we both might have to accept that there is nothing more we can do, not when other people are so determined to stand in our way. For our own sense of peace and for your sister's and mine, my mother, and even my stubborn father's. I wish I did not find myself doubting that clinging to the dream that ours will be a story with a happy ending is doing rather more harm than not. Sometimes, we must put the well-being of those we love above our own. I know you would for your sister, and I would never blame you. How would she feel to have her family torn asunder, to say nothing of your cousins and aunts and uncles?" She kissed his hand, lightly touched his cheek, and, as she backed away, whispered, "Goodbye."

Shaking his head, he said, "Only for now, *not* forever."

Her smile appeared both resolute, as though she believed him, and wistful, giving the impression that she was afraid to. "For now." She then turned about and strode away.

As Elizabeth walked to Longbourn, she hoped the cool morning air would help to mask the signs of her sorrow. Her cheeks burned, and she could do nothing to prevent the tears that covered them; it was a miracle she managed not to sob. How she had prayed Mr Darcy would tell her everything with his family had been resolved! But he had not, and so, she had been forced to tell him of her father's determination to refuse his consent. As difficult as it had been, she knew it was better that she be the one to explain rather than allow the gentlemen to discuss it, certain it would make the situation worse, perhaps cause a permanent breach between them that would make it impossible for her and Mr Darcy to reunite if his family ceased their objections, as she fervently hoped they would. As it was, she had delayed admitting what her father had said, though why she had wanted to protect him she did not know.

Perhaps it is simply because I do not want Mr Darcy to hate Papa. She would not blame him, to be sure, and she even understood why his opinion of her family—save the Gardiners and Jane—was not particularly good. The more animosity between her father and the man she longed to marry, the more threatened her future happiness was.

She had been desperate to take in everything about Mr Darcy—his looks, the faint odour of his cologne, the sense of his presence, the sound of his voice. If only she could imprint it all in her memory, because she was horribly afraid she would never be that near to him again, especially not alone. She did her best to watch him every moment they were together, but looking away had been necessary to prevent herself from behaving impetuously. How she had wanted to throw herself into his arms and beg him not to let anything or anyone come between them, no matter what they had to do or tolerate to be together.

But she could not forget their loved ones. She had meant what she had said about giving him the gift of his family, and as much as she wanted a life with him, a portion of her joy, of her ability to be the wife he deserved, might be lost to her grief at the consequences. Marrying without her father's consent or blessing would rob her of their connexion, and should Jane suffer in any way because of her actions, she would never forgive herself.

Once at Longbourn, she went to her chamber and did her best to repair the damage to her features caused by her interview with Mr Darcy before joining her family at breakfast. Fortunately, Mr Bingley would be here all day. Jane would thus be occupied with him. It might allow Elizabeth to hide how wretchedly she felt. In time, she would learn to mask her heartache from the world.

If it became necessary. Elizabeth had tried her best to discourage Mr Darcy as her father had demanded she do, and every word she had said to him was the truth. Yet, she could not, would not, be quick to give up on the possibility that he would find a way out of their present dilemma. *And I shall be ready to do my part, whatever is necessary!* Likely, it would start with arguing her father into giving his blessing, and she was resolved to do just that.

CHAPTER EIGHT

Darcy watched Elizabeth walk away until the path curved and he could no longer see her. With each second, two emotions surged to ever greater heights within: anger and determination. Elizabeth might not know how to act, but *he* did. She might struggle to hope, but he did not. He understood why she did; the blame must be shared by her father and his aunts and uncle, Lady Catherine most of all. To be sure, Darcy reluctantly understood Mr Bennet's reservations, but the man had made a decision that would profoundly affect his daughter's happiness and well-being forever without any pause or even asking *him* what he was doing to address his family's objections. Darcy could and would act; he would ensure that he and Elizabeth had their happily ever after.

His return to Netherfield was as fast as it could be without him actually running. Once there, he learnt from the butler than Bingley had already left for Longbourn; everyone else was in the drawing room.

"Very good," Darcy said to the servant, relieved to know his family was all in one place. It would make his task that much easier. "Please have my valet informed to prepare to depart as soon as possible."

He entered the drawing room with the storm inside reaching its zenith. It would take effort to contain it, but for Elizabeth's sake, he would. Nothing would be served by telling Lady Catherine and Lord Romsley what he presently thought of them.

"There you are, Darcy! Where have you been?" Lady Catherine demanded.

"We are leaving. *All* of us. This morning," he said in a tone that would brook no disagreement. He refused to respond to his aunt, even when she repeated herself. To no great surprise, there were many exclamations, but he overlooked them. "This has gone on far too long. You may not have noticed, but Bingley has—yet again—left his house before breakfast. *His* house, to which *none* of you were invited. I refuse to put him in the position of having to host this disgusting family reunion any longer."

"Nephew, have a care," the earl warned.

"He is right, Father," Fitzwilliam said.

"I concur," Bramwell added. "It was ill-advised, at best."

The countess said something to Lord Romsley that Darcy did not hear, and he continued to pretend that his other aunt was not present. Anne sat silently beside her mother, only the pink spots on her face and lowered chin suggested she was paying attention to the conversation.

"Where are you planning to go?" Fitzwilliam asked.

"Pemberley. I have business in London too, but first, I must go home." Georgiana was there, and he wished to talk to her.

Lady Catherine made a loud noise that could only be called a snort. "You must think me a fool if you believe you can trick me this way. You may get into your carriage and even take the road north for a short while, but then you will return here and allow yourself to be trapped by that girl!"

I do not believe you to be a fool. I know *you are, if you think I shall live my life according to your wishes!*

Bramwell laughed, presumably at her words, which earned him a reprimand from his father. At the same time, the countess said, "Really, Catherine, you take this too far."

"Your son, the future Earl of Romsley, wants to marry a solicitor's daughter," Lady Catherine said. "You can have nothing useful to say of proper comportment. *My* daughter was raised to follow her duty."

"Do not speak to my wife in that manner! As for Bramwell, you will keep your opinion to yourself," his uncle said.

Fitzwilliam caught Darcy's eye and grimaced, his expression one of sympathy, as he so often appeared when they were in company with Lady Catherine. Bramwell sighed loudly and said, "With each word that is spoken, we are only proving that my cousin is correct. We have been here—and together—too long."

"Are you including yourself in that?" the colonel said with feigned humour.

"Naturally," Bramwell replied.

At the same time, Lady Romsley said, "It is time for us to return to town." To her husband, she added, "Do you not agree?"

He nodded.

"I am resolved to remain where I am until Darcy agrees to marry Anne and returns to Kent with us!" Lady Catherine stated.

Darcy wondered if she was as fatigued of saying the words as he was of listening to them. From the expressions worn by everyone apart from Anne, he suspected they were thinking likewise.

"I am going to Pemberley," he repeated. "I shall ensure Bingley knows that I would not blame him if he had you forcibly ejected, should you refuse to leave on your own."

This naturally caused several rather indignant responses, although he had the impression his uncle did not object as much as he was attempting to sound. The earl said, "Catherine, return to Rosings. Anne looks like she needs to be home. It is what you want, is it not, Niece?"

Anne nodded meekly; Lady Catherine glared at her.

"Margaret and I shall go to town," Lord Romsley added. "Bramwell will go with us. I have not forgotten that we have a serious conversation to finish about his future. Fitzwilliam, what will you do?"

The colonel looked between his brother and Darcy before saying, "I shall go to Derbyshire, if my cousin does not object."

"Good thinking, Brother!" The viscount grinned at him. "You can ensure he does not sneak back to Meryton to fall under—"

"Bramwell!" the earl barked, ending his eldest son's joke.

At another time, Darcy might have found the scene humorous; at present, all he could do was think of the tasks ahead of him and his desire to begin them at once. Accordingly, he reiterated that he expected they would all be in their carriages and driving away from Hertfordshire by noon, then left the room.

The morning following Elizabeth's conversation with Mr Darcy, Mr Bingley arrived at Longbourn soon after breakfast.

"I had to meet with the steward," he said. Glancing at Elizabeth, he gave an awkward laugh that left her wondering if Mr Darcy had told him of their conversation the previous day. "There always seems to be so much to do. Not that I mind!" he added hastily. "Indeed, I find that the more I become familiar with the business of managing an estate, the more satisfying I find it."

"And I am very sure you excel at it," Mrs Bennet said.

"Netherfield has never had a more deserving master. Is that not right, Jane?" Regardless of Jane's engagement, their mother continued to push the couple together just as she had when she had been anxiously awaiting the moment he would propose.

Thank goodness she never noticed Mr Darcy's interest in me! Elizabeth reflected. As horrible as her present circumstances were, they would be so much more difficult if she had to explain to her mother why he had gone away yet again. With her attention on the upcoming wedding, her mother had not even commented on Mr Bingley's unexpected guests other than saying she supposed there was some important family business they needed to discuss with Mr Darcy. Since she had not learnt to think well of him—which she undoubtedly would have the instant Elizabeth announced their betrothal—she had no time to spare on speculating about his activities.

A short while later, Mr Bingley and Elizabeth were able to speak alone. They sat in one corner of the drawing room near the window, while her sisters chatted with Mrs Bennet.

"I hardly know what to say." His voice was quiet, but not quite a whisper, and he glanced towards the ladies. Elizabeth did likewise and saw that Kitty was speaking with particular animation.

"I believe they are safely occupied and will not intrude," she said. "Please tell me whatever you think I should know."

He sighed and nodded. "There is really very little. It is

only that...when I returned to Netherfield last evening, I found the house empty. Darcy and his relations are gone. I understand from the butler that they left at about noon. He—Darcy that is—left a note for me, but he only wrote that he was going to Pemberley and offered an apology for how his family had shown up without any warning whatsoever. That, obviously, is not a matter I care about. Well,"—his features briefly contorted as though he was carefully considering the point— "I suppose I did care, but Darcy had no role in it."

"I understand," she said before he could continue. "I am sure you are very glad to have your home to yourself again. For the moment, that is. Jane mentioned that your sisters and Mr Hurst would be coming soon. When do you expect them?" She asked not out of interest, but rather to divert his attention to anything other than Mr Darcy. Sure enough, her ploy worked. Since the reason for the Hursts and Miss Bingley's journey was to celebrate his engagement and wedding, he spoke of Jane and his happiness for as long as Elizabeth could bear to listen.

Fortunately, her patience ended just when her father returned from making a call. As was his habit, he stuck his head into the room to inform them he was at home, only opening the door wide enough to permit it. When he spied her, he paused, then walked over to her and Mr Bingley, who leapt to his feet.

"Good morning, sir!" Mr Bingley said jovially. "You see me trespassing on your hospitality yet again. Or should I say your excellent wife's?"

Mr Bennet chuckled. "If you behaved any differently,

I might wonder at the depths of your attachment to my Jane. You may return to my eldest daughter. I have need of Lizzy."

Mr Bingley grinned and did as his future father-in-law suggested. Elizabeth watched him cross the room before turning to her father. She arched her brow in question.

"Give me a quarter of an hour, then meet me in my book-room," he said.

Still, she did not speak; she nodded and did her utmost not to show that she disliked the prospect, suspecting he wanted to talk about Mr Darcy. Beyond that, he must know she was not in good spirits. Although he had been gone before breakfast and had not seen her after her sleepless night—the second in a row—he could not miss how pale and listless she was. Her mother had spoken of it earlier, and Elizabeth had claimed a headache. Fortunately, Jane had distracted their mother with some piece of neighbourhood gossip, ensuring she did not enquire into her second daughter's indisposition further.

When Elizabeth and Mr Bennet were in the book-room, a tray of tea and biscuits sitting on the desk between them, he regarded her steadily for a long moment before speaking.

"You are unhappy," he said. "I suppose you spoke to him?"

"Mr Darcy?" she asked, although there was little doubt whom he meant. She was delaying, dreading he would insist she recount the interview in detail, not realising how each second of memory was like a stab to the very core of her being. Only after he nodded did she continue. "Yesterday."

"Did Mr Bingley bring some message from him? Is that why the pair of you were sitting alone when we all know he prefers not to leave Jane's side, even when it is necessary? Ah, to be young and in love." He rolled his eyes, but if he thought Elizabeth was in a mood to laugh or joke, especially about love, he was much mistaken.

"No. He wanted to tell me that all his guests departed yesterday morning. Are you satisfied, Papa? He is gone, and you need not worry about upsetting Lord Romsley." There was no hiding the bitterness in her tone, and one of Mr Bennet's eyebrows rose up his forehead. Once upon, a time, Elizabeth had wished she could move her brows independently as he did; currently, she dreamt of plucking out each of the hairs in his one by one.

It was possible, nay, it seemed certain, that she resented him for forcing her to break with Mr Darcy. If they found a way to reunite, she *might* forgive Mr Bennet.

"You are unhappy," he said again, this time with what sounded like genuine sympathy. It almost brought tears to her eyes, but if she let them form, he would seek to comfort her, and that she could not abide. "I had not expected to find you quite so miserable, but I can see that you are."

She shrugged and kept her gaze on the teacup she held in her lap. It remained full of milky tea, but she could not bring herself to drink it.

"I had no notion your feelings for him were…this substantial."

With a bark of humourless laughter, she glanced at him and said, "They are. Indeed, they are everything they should be for a man I expected and wanted to marry."

She heard a deep, slow sigh, but otherwise, there was a long moment of silence before he spoke. "I am sorry, Lizzy. I trust you take my lack of teasing as an indication of my sincerity. What choice did I have? No, do not answer," he said, although she had done nothing to suggest she would. "I had to act in a manner I believed was in the best interest of you and our family."

Again, neither of them spoke. A single thought occupied her mind: Mr Darcy was gone. What should she make of it? *That he can no longer bear to be near me when I have told him there is no future for us? Dear Lord, how could I have done so?* She knew why, but it seemed so improbable that she had managed to stand across from him and say the words. Yesterday, she had wanted to remember everything about him, and she had succeeded; at present, she could recall only too vividly the devastation in his eyes as she informed him she would not marry him without her father's approval.

Clearing her throat, she placed the dish on the desk and stood. "Do not concern yourself. I shall recover in time, once I remember I am not formed for unhappiness." She offered him a small, meaningless smile and left the room.

It was not entirely a lie. If she was forced to, she would find a way to be content without Mr Darcy, but she preferred another explanation for why he had departed so hastily that he had not even waited to speak to his friend. *Dare I hope that even now, he is working to convince his family to change their opinion of me and our union?* She did, of course; she could not do otherwise, knowing the sort of gentleman he was and accepting the depths of his affection for her. During his absence, which she prayed would not be of long duration, she would speak to her father of Mr Darcy, to teach him to know the man she had come to love with everything that she was.

CHAPTER NINE

At Darcy's insistence, he and Fitzwilliam made the trip to Derbyshire as quickly as possible, taking advantage of each possible hour of daylight. In the carriage, he talked through his strategy with his cousin, and when they stopped for the night, he wrote letters, most necessarily to the solicitors his father had typically consulted, but also the earl and many to Elizabeth. The latter were filled with explanations of what he was doing, reassurances that he would succeed and meet the implied demands of her father, and expressions of his deep, never-ending love. He might not be able to send them to her, but he would give them to her eventually, once they were married. Knowing her as he did, in the future, she would find a way to laugh at everything that was causing them such anxiety currently and making him feel as though he were ageing a decade each hour. *And she will make me laugh at it too*, he reflected with wonder. She was astonishing in all the best ways.

Before parting at Netherfield, Darcy had asked Lord Romsley if he was truly willing to cause a breach by refusing to accept Darcy's right to make his own decisions.

The earl had retorted, "Are *you* willing to risk it over this girl? Are you so infatuated with her that you do not care how much distress your union might cause?"

Darcy's answer had been swift and decisive. "I *do* love her that much, but this is not just about her. It is about your interference. As much as I respect you and do not want to quarrel, I cannot accept you or Lady Catherine telling me what I may and may not do."

Writing to him currently, Darcy reiterated his stance, doing his best to calmly and clearly express why Elizabeth was the lady he wanted as his wife and why he was so resolved. He knew he had not been as eloquent on the matter when they were at Netherfield; he had been too stunned, and it never was particularly easy for him to express himself when speaking, as his first proposal to Elizabeth had demonstrated all too well.

Fitzwilliam reviewed the letter and approved. "I am convinced my parents will see reason. I understand from my mother that our aunt told them you, she, and Anne had agreed to an autumnal wedding when we were in Kent together. I assured her I knew nothing of it and asked if she genuinely thought you would jilt Anne, which—for your information—she does not." He rolled his eyes. "She and Father only need to be away from Lady Catherine and take a few moments to reflect."

"That is what I believe—or want to believe," Darcy

said. "Especially if I can assure them that I have searched through my father's papers and consulted his solicitors and can find no evidence that he was that intent on me marrying Anne."

Unspoken was that, for himself, and to assure Elizabeth, he had to know what his father had really thought. Was Lady Catherine correct that the union had been his father's express desire? Had he lived, would he have done his best to convince Darcy to agree, even to demand he do so? *I refuse to accept that he would have, knowing how little I liked the prospect!* Likewise, he truly believed his father would have approved of Elizabeth, especially knowing how happy she made him.

Darcy had sent word to Georgiana to expect them, thus their arrival Saturday night was not a surprise in itself. Yet, he had offered no explanation for his trip or Fitzwilliam's reason for coming with him, and it was evident that his sister understood something significant had happened. As he and his cousin ate a late dinner, she sat with them, her gaze continually shifting between them, but resting most often on him, her hands clasped together and resting on top of the fine mahogany table. They spoke of the roads, the weather they had encountered, and which inns they had stayed at, the conversation stilted. Only after they had finished eating did he and Fitzwilliam inform her of recent events in Meryton. Her mouth hung open inelegantly.

"But why would they act so-so—?" she cried. "Miss Elizabeth is lovely and kind."

"You know Lady Catherine's hopes," Fitzwilliam said gently.

Georgiana nodded impatiently. "But my brother has never wanted to marry Anne! They must know that."

"Know and accept are very different matters." As he spoke, Darcy stood and began to slowly pace about the room. He was agitated, longing to leap into the tasks he had planned, but recognising the importance of speaking to his sister.

"Poor Miss Elizabeth," she said. Her eyes were round and bright with tears and, as he walked by her, he briefly stopped to kiss the top of her head. "You will not give up, will you?" she asked. "Surely, our aunt and uncle Romsley can be made to accept her."

"I think so," Fitzwilliam said. "Your brother has an idea or two regarding them, but especially how to clip Lady Catherine's wings, so to speak."

Georgiana stood and regarded him. "How? Please let me help you, Brother!"

Darcy smiled and, stepping towards her, took her by the shoulders. "I am very glad to hear you say that. You, my dear, are part of my plan."

For the next hour or so, they drank tea and discussed what Darcy had expected to accomplish by coming to Pemberley. His stay would not be long, and they agreed that, when he travelled south again in a few days, Georgiana and her companion, as well as Fitzwilliam, would go with him. In the meantime, his sister and cousin would do whatever they could to assist him. What that mostly involved was reading through old papers of his father's that had not been destroyed after his death. Hugh Darcy had kept everything—letters, notebooks in which he recorded his activities and lists of items he wished to attend to so that he would not forget, to say nothing of information related to important business matters. Darcy had looked through the latter out of necessity soon after his father's death, but in his grief, he had not the strength to read the more personal records. It was these, in particular, that they searched, looking for anything he had written regarding his son's marriage, either to Anne de Bourgh or more generally. Darcy used part of his time to consult with several people who lived locally, notably the vicar and a neighbour his father had considered a close friend. None of them could recall his father ever speaking of the matter, certainly not of referring to Anne—or any other lady—as the future Mrs Darcy.

Late Tuesday afternoon, the three of them concluded that they had accomplished all they could at Pemberley and should depart for London the next day.

"You should be satisfied with what we have discovered," Fitzwilliam said when Darcy expressed frustration; he gave his cousin a sceptical look in response.

"He is correct," Georgiana insisted. "I think that, if Papa had truly wanted you to marry Anne, he would have told someone. Yet, you have uncovered nothing like that. Mrs Reynolds cannot recall any offhanded remarks, and Papa certainly would have mentioned it in relation to redecorating rooms or the like. They often spoke of such matters. And if he had written to Uncle Darcy or one of his friends about his supposed intentions, there would have been a hint of it in their letters. Although I would not like to say Lady Catherine was less than truthful, none of her letters to Papa make mention of the marriage contract she claimed they were discussing."

"When did you become so wise?" he asked.

She blushed and shyly averted her eyes. "It is only that I very, very much want you to marry Miss Elizabeth. I know she will make you happy and, although I know this is horribly selfish to say, I do so want her to be my sister."

"Say exactly that, and in the same manner, to my mother and father, and they will drop all opposition to her becoming your brother's wife," Fitzwilliam said.

Unfortunately, Lady Catherine would not be so easy to convince. *I shall threaten her, if necessary!* Darcy thought, accepting the bitterness in his reflections as her due.

Darcy remained awake long after his cousin and sister retired, again writing letters, one to inform the earl of what they had discovered—or failed to—and the other to Elizabeth. He would send the former by express, permitting the earl and countess time to contemplate the situation carefully before he next spoke to them in person, which would be soon after he arrived in town. The latter missive was added to the collection he would present to Elizabeth. He imagined the two of them sitting on a sofa in the mistress's chamber, his arms wrapped around her, as she read his words, of how wonderful it would feel to finally be free to love her as she deserved.

Before that happy day was possible, he must gain his family's approval—reluctant or enthusiastic, he did not care—and he felt more confident than ever that he would. After all, there was no proof that his father would have insisted he marry Anne, no basis for supposing that he was honour-bound to his cousin, apart from the oft-repeated wishes of her mother. He was free to marry where he liked. And there would be little gossip about Elizabeth being an imprudent match, so long as his relations showed they accepted her as Mrs Darcy. Once his family agreed, all that would be left was assuring Mr Bennet that there were no more impediments, and then—for the third and, he trusted, final time—he would propose to Elizabeth.

Elizabeth did her best to attend to her usual activities despite being increasingly distracted each day, wondering where Mr Darcy was and whether—when—she would see him again. Several times, her mother asked if she was unwell, but she was easily satisfied by Elizabeth's assurances that she was not. Her father attempted to console her once or twice, but Elizabeth found little comfort in his company. If she was a different sort of woman, she would tell him that she blamed him for not—at the least—delaying his decision regarding Mr Darcy. Without speaking to the gentleman, and perhaps the earl or some other of his family, her father had decided he would not support a marriage between her and the man she loved.

It mattered not that she understood and even reluctantly agreed with part of his concern. Instead of accepting his assurances that he had acted in her best interests, Elizabeth told him that he was mistaken about Mr Darcy, who was an excellent gentleman, and she was as resolved to marry him as he was to marry her. Displaying confidence, she asked him to be prepared to reconsider his opinion when Mr Darcy returned with proof the situation with his family had been resolved. She was not quite as certain that day would arrive as she let on, although she mostly was; fear of losing what they might have had—either because of his family or her father's refusal—made it impossible to banish the last iota of doubt.

Keeping her vexation, anxiety, and disappointment secret was difficult, but she smiled and laughed, and rejoiced in Jane's happiness to the best of her ability.

The situation had one benefit: she and Mr Bingley became better friends. He took the time to talk to her, brought her into his conversations with her elder sister, attempted to amuse her, and so forth. And he spoke to her of Mr Darcy.

"I know you will not ask, but there was no letter from Darcy today. I did not expect one, necessarily, especially if he has no news to share. I have known him many years, as I suppose you know?" Mr Bingley said one evening. They were at Purvis Lodge and were sitting together in the drawing room after dinner. Jane was at his other side, chatting with Maria Lucas.

"Yes," Elizabeth said with a slight smile. That Mr Darcy had not yet written his friend left her with a hollow sensation in her belly. "He told me of your meeting at school as boys."

"When he became my mentor and—I do not think he knows this, and it is a bit embarrassing—the example I followed to become a gentleman, as my father wished me to be. He is a good man, the best I know."

Her smile was more heartfelt this time. "I think so too."

"To be sure, he has his flaws and makes mistakes, just as we all do." His eyes drifted to Jane momentarily before he returned his attention to Elizabeth. "I know you are aware of his and my sisters' interference with..." He indicated her sister, and when she nodded, he continued. "He told me you did when we spoke of it. That was a long conversation, but during it, I learnt some important lessons, mainly to trust my own opinion more." He shook himself. "What I wanted to say is that he does not give his friendship or confidence easily, and I have never heard him even hint that he had a special regard for any lady. That he does for you assures me he has given you his loyalty along with his devotion. He will not soon forget, and he will not stop his efforts to convince his relations that he is making the best possible choice of wife. I know you are well suited. Jane and I had spoken of how much we would like to see the two of you form an attachment and then, to our astonishment, we discovered that you had!" He laughed. "I shall do whatever I can to help, although I do not really know what I might actually do."

Elizabeth lightly lay her hand on his arm in a gesture

of gratitude and affection. "I have struggled with the same question, longed to discover some step I might take, and have failed to find an answer. Thank you, and please permit me to tell you again how glad I am you will be my brother. I could not imagine one better."

At that moment, the pianoforte was opened, and Elizabeth was asked to play, effectively ending their conversation.

CHAPTER TEN

About one week after Mr Darcy's departure, Elizabeth was sitting at home with her mother, sisters, and Mr Bingley; Mr Bennet was gone to Hertford for the day on business. Suddenly, Kitty, who was looking out the window and complaining about the lack of activity, cried out.

"The most magnificent carriage is coming up the drive! It is not like the last one, that lady who lives near Charlotte. This one is even bigger and more elegant. Who could it be?" She turned her eager eyes to her family, evidently expecting one of them to offer an explanation.

Elizabeth's mouth was too dry to speak, and her heart beat wildly in her chest. Might it be one of Mr Darcy's relations? Might it be the gentleman himself, possibly in a carriage Kitty had not seen before.

"Jane and I were about to..." Mr Bingley said, pointing towards the door. His voice drew Elizabeth's attention.

"But perhaps we should stay," Jane added, watching her closely.

She understood they wanted to go into the gardens to be alone for a while; they had indeed mentioned it just minutes ago.

"It is fine," she said quietly so that only they heard. "Whoever it is, whatever they have to say, I shall be well."

No one else was paying attention to them. Kitty and Mrs Bennet were speculating on who their caller was, and Mary was tidying the table at which she had been working. Elizabeth was aware that she, Mr Bingley, and Jane were assuming the visitor had come to see her. It was not a surprise that her mother and younger sisters did not; they were ignorant of recent events regarding her, Mr Darcy, and his family. She swallowed her anxiety, reassured Jane again, and the couple slipped out of the room in time to avoid greeting the caller.

Elizabeth was not sure whom she anticipated would enter the drawing room. If she had a longer period of reflection, she might have considered the persons involved, but at present, all she could do was push aside the unpleasant memories of her encounter with Lady Catherine at Longbourn and what she had witnessed at Netherfield when that lady and her relations had come to confront Mr Darcy. *I shall remain calm and polite,* she vowed, *but I shall not accept being mistreated. Courage, Lizzy!*

Just then, the Countess of Romsley was announced. The lady stood by the door, her expensive, fashionable attire a stark contrast to the room's décor. Elizabeth had never considered it lacking, but with Lady Romsley there, it appeared worn and faded. The woman was lovely and must have been one of the most noted beauties of the *ton* when she had entered society. Currently, her eyes took in the room, but from what Elizabeth could discern, her gaze was not especially critical. The countess smiled politely and her expression was open.

"My lady," Mrs Bennet said, curtseying deeply. "Girls, girls," she continued, whispering loudly, her eyes darting between her daughters and their guest, suggesting she was reminding them to mind their manners. Glancing at her sisters, Elizabeth saw that Kitty was gaping at the countess, and Mary was unable to disguise her curiosity and wariness. She did not know if they knew of the connexion between Lady Romsley and Mr Darcy, and, naturally, they would have no notion why she might be there.

"Lady Romsley," Elizabeth said, though she might not have been heard, given how her mother had begun to babble—there was no other word for it—directing the countess to the best chair, talking about refreshments, the weather, and Elizabeth knew not what else. She was too caught by the woman's bright blue eyes, which rested on her.

"You are very kind, Mrs Bennet, especially since I have called so unexpectedly," Lady Romsley said, her voice warm. "You must be wondering why."

It seldom happened that her mother had nothing to

say, but at this moment, she remained silent and stared at her caller, her lips parted.

"Mama," Elizabeth said, "Lady Romsley is Mr Darcy's aunt. Her husband is Lady Catherine's brother."

"Oh, Lady Catherine!" Mrs Bennet cried, and for a moment spoke about Mr Collins's connexion to the lady and her being so generous as to bring Elizabeth a letter from Mrs Collins a fortnight earlier. All the while, Lady Romsley sat and listened attentively, nodding and making the appropriate sounds. She also glanced at Elizabeth repeatedly.

"Oh, where is the tea?" her mother said, looking about the room as though it might be hiding in a corner. "Mary, ask Mrs Hill. Now, child."

"While I would certainly enjoy a cup, please do not concern yourself with any delay. Indeed, I have not noticed one at all," Lady Romsley said. "I wonder if, while we wait, I might have a moment alone with Miss Elizabeth?"

Elizabeth refused to look at her mother and sisters, but she could feel their eyes on her. Even in the quiet of the room, she heard their enquiries. What had *she* to do with the countess? Why would another of Mr Darcy's relations seek her out? She stood, regarded the lady, and said, "We might go into the parlour, if that would suit you?"

Lady Romsley agreed, and, pretending not to hear the whispers of Mrs Bennet, Mary, and Kitty, Elizabeth led her into the smaller room that was usually reserved for the family; her mother would fret about a countess seeing the older furnishings, and Elizabeth would have to reassure her while also evading her questions about their conversation.

"Come sit with me," Lady Romsley said. She went to a faded brocade settee and patted the place next to her.

Elizabeth did as directed, and regarded her steadily, waiting for her to say what she wished. The lady's air was almost but not quite serene, which was puzzling. When Lady Catherine had called, it was evident from the outset that she was displeased and her visit would be a trial, but Elizabeth did not have the same sense with Lady Romsley. Assuming she had come from town, she must have left extremely early—possibly as the sun was rising.

"You must be wondering why I am here," the countess said, repeating her earlier words to Mrs Bennet. "I shall explain, though so much has happened this past week, I might need to apologise for not being as eloquent as I would like. I am sure you realise it is about my nephew."

Seeing that some response was needed, Elizabeth nodded. "I had assumed. I hope he and all of your family are well." There was a slight tremor in her voice that she hated; it denoted weakness, and she had no wish to display such an emotion at present.

"Oh, yes, everyone is perfectly well. I ought to have said so at once to spare you any anxiety. Are you? The scene at Mr Bingley's estate last week must have been distressing to you. Am I correct that your mother is unaware of...?"

"She is, and I am well. Thank you for asking, my

lady." Because she was bracing herself for whatever came next, she found it difficult to speak.

Lady Romsley nodded. "Very well. First, let me tell you where we all went and what we did. My husband insisted his sister and niece return to Rosings, and to my surprise, Catherine obeyed him. The earl, Bramwell, and I went to town. My son wishes to marry Miss Rebecca Darcy, the paternal cousin of my nephew. It is not the match we envisioned for Bramwell, but..." She gave a light laugh. "We had such peaceful lives, the earl and I occasionally speaking of our sons and nephew and their need for wives, and suddenly, we are embroiled in discussions and debates because two of them—I meant to include Fitzwilliam as well, you see, though, fortunately, he has no immediate interest in matrimony—have acted in ways we did not anticipate, shall we say?"

And do you hate your son's choice as much as your nephew's? Are you telling him he must marry a lady you have decided upon? Elizabeth would not dare to ask the questions aloud.

"Fitzwilliam went with Darcy to Pemberley. We have had several letters from my nephew. Darcy has been searching through his father's old papers and speaking to his old friends. I understand he has also written to the solicitors. It is all part of his effort to disprove Lady Catherine's claims that my brother-in-law expected him to marry Anne. He had a great deal to say about you, as well, and our belief that we can interfere in his life. The last was directed at the earl, but I must take some of it on myself, because I did try to convince him to set you aside and marry Anne. Darcy is not entirely wrong that we have no right to tell him what to do, but neither is he entirely correct. He *is* part of our family, and what he does affects us. But I admit the way we have handled the situation was not kind or conducive to rational discussion. We received a letter from Fitzwilliam yesterday. He informed us that he and Darcy will soon be in London. I believe Georgiana travels with them."

The countess paused and studied Elizabeth for a long moment, her head tilted to one side. "I realised that, as much as we spoke *of* you, we knew very little *about* you. To be sure, my sister-in-law spent time with you when you were visiting her parson's wife. I ought not to call the man Catherine's parson, but knowing how she seeks to control everyone near her"—she laughed to herself—"which might be one reason Darcy does not want to marry Anne."

Yet again not knowing what to say, Elizabeth continued to hold her tongue. She kept her hands tightly clasped in her lap to stop herself from fidgeting; it felt like a horde of little insects was crawling across her back.

"You will not be surprised to know that Catherine told us a great deal about you, and I shall not lie. It did... shock and concern the earl and me. Our coming to Hertfordshire was the decision of a moment, and largely at her insistence. It was only later that I began to wonder how much was exaggeration and what you were actually like. Forgive me if this sounds too harsh, but if my husband and I are going to continue arguing against my nephew marrying you, I would like to know that *I* have reasons for it, ones I have decided myself and not because someone whose opinion I do not trust has said I should. This situation is too serious, the consequences too important, not to be more careful than I have been thus far."

Elizabeth cleared her throat and forced her features to remain impassive; she was taken aback but thought it impolite to show it. Even more, she was not sure she wanted the countess to understand what she was feeling. "That is generous of your ladyship. It is true that Lady Catherine did not much like what I told her of myself and my family when I was in Kent, and..."

"Pray, continue, my dear," Lady Romsley said when Elizabeth pressed her lips together.

After a brief debate, she said, "I suspect Mr Collins of telling her whatever news of my family he receives and embellishing our flaws, perhaps mine especially."

"Because..." Her brow arched.

"I rejected his offer of marriage, knowing I would never be happy with him, and, as a consequence, he would likely be unhappy too. He was deeply insulted. As my father's heir, I suspect he assumed he could take his pick of me and my sisters. I know it would have been a prudent match, but it was impossible." She believed the vignette would demonstrate something of her character, which is why she had shared such a personal memory.

The countess made a noise of interest and slowly nodded, keeping her gaze on Elizabeth. "Catherine says you have no fortune and your mother's connexions are in trade. I do not recall my nephew saying otherwise."

"She was correct. My father has no living relatives apart from Mr Collins, my mother's sister is married to a solicitor in Meryton, and her brother is a businessman with warehouses in Cheapside."

Her companion sighed. "I would be happier if your family circumstances were better. I cannot deny such things are important in our society. You must realise that, whether you—or I—agree with it or not. My nephew's mother was the daughter of an earl and brought a substantial fortune to her marriage. We were not wrong to suppose his wife would have a similar background."

"How unfortunate he did not fall in love with such a lady," Elizabeth said, regretting the words immediately. Her cheeks burned, and she lowered her chin, chastising herself.

Lady Romsley touched her hand, and her voice was calm and comforting. "Darcy has insisted that he knows what he is about. He told us that his feelings are of long duration and that you are everything perfect."

Elizabeth chuckled. "The first two are true, especially the second, but as for my supposed perfection, that was far more generous than I deserve. Your nephew knows full well that I am not."

Lady Romsley also laughed. "It is just as well. I have never met a man or woman who believed their spouse was perfect before marriage who managed to still be happy afterwards. Eventually, the shine wears off, and usually very quickly. Amongst his protestations that you are caring and intelligent and diligent and well-mannered, and I know not what else, Darcy also said this or that—I cannot recall exactly what—that left me believing he not only is in love with you, and I do believe he is, but that he simply enjoys being in your company. I find great reassurance in that. The strongest unions are ones where the couple are friends as well as lovers. You are a very pretty young woman, all the more when you blush, and you have such lovely eyes. No doubt, that is what first drew his attention, but there is much more to you. Tell me about yourself. What do you like to do?"

They spoke for some time. It did not take long for Elizabeth to ease, and she was as open with the countess as possible, sensing her approval and affection for Mr Darcy. They spoke briefly of Lydia's marriage to Mr Wickham, her companion seemingly relieved to know the couple were living in Newcastle, no one in the neighbourhood was gossiping about the unfortunate beginning to their marriage, and that Elizabeth had no interest in spending time with them. Possibly, Lady Romsley would cease to object to her nephew's interest in Elizabeth. *If she can convince the earl to do likewise, I* could *coax my father into giving his consent. Then, all would be as it was supposed to be!*

Eventually, they returned to the drawing room. Jane and Mr Bingley had come inside, and the party enjoyed tea and a light repast. Mr Bingley invited Lady Romsley to stay at Netherfield Park that night.

"You might prefer it to returning to town this afternoon," he said.

"That is generous of you," she replied. "However, I must decline. My husband would worry. If I leave now, I might just make it to town before it grows full dark." Addressing Elizabeth, she added, "I look forward to seeing you again soon, my dear." To Mrs Bennet, she said, "You have a charming daughter. Indeed, you have been blessed with many."

Mrs Bennet thanked her, evidently flustered, and peered at Elizabeth, no doubt confused and curious by the day's happenings.

The countess turned to Jane and said, "Miss Bennet, I am afraid I have not had a chance to offer you my congratulations on your betrothal. I do hope you will call on me when you are in town."

Jane blushed. "Thank you, your ladyship. That is very kind of you."

Lady Romsley smiled broadly, taking in Jane, Mr Bingley, and Elizabeth. "I would say it is also practical of me. I anticipate another happy event will occur soon, and it will ensure we meet often in town. My nephew and Mr Bingley are such good friends." She chuckled and rolled her eyes, which made her look much less imposing. "Mr Hurst is also some sort of cousin to me, twice or thrice removed, but I always seem to forget that. Well, I must be off. Mrs Bennet, thank you very much for your hospitality. Please tell your husband I am sorry not to have seen him too." She curtseyed and nodded politely to everyone, reserving a final smile for Elizabeth; she also patted her cheek.

There was a long silence after she was gone. Elizabeth watched the door, but she heard someone shuffling their feet—Mr Bingley, she thought—and the antique long case clock keeping time.

At length, Mrs Bennet said, "Lizzy, what has happened?"

On the brink of tears she could not explain, Elizabeth hastily excused herself and ran from the room.

CHAPTER ELEVEN

Darcy and his companions arrived in town at the dinner hour on Thursday. It was too late to call on either of his uncles that night, although he was eager to accomplish the next step in his plan so that he might finally become an engaged man. Instead, he ensured his sister was properly settled after their journey and reviewed the responses to the letters he had sent out asking for information about his father's intentions—or even hopes—for his future. Everything he had learnt led to only one possible conclusion: Hugh Darcy may have considered a union between his son and niece prudent, given Anne's fortune and because it would strengthen the connexion between the Darcys and de Bourghs, but he had taken no steps to prepare for it. Nor was there proof that he would have insisted on it, had he lived.

The following morning, Darcy went to see his uncle Frederick Darcy. If anyone would know of his father's wishes for the future, it was Frederick; the brothers had always been close. His aunt and cousin were out, and while Darcy regretted not seeing them, it was his uncle with whom he most needed to speak. Even though Frederick had heard something of the situation with Elizabeth, Lady Catherine, and his other maternal relations, Darcy reviewed it, providing more details than Bramwell had when he had called two days ago.

"I searched through all my father's papers, wrote to the solicitors he used, even spoke to the vicar in Derbyshire. I can find nothing to suggest that he was going to tell me I must marry my cousin, or even that it was more than a vague wish of his and my mother's," Darcy said. "Did he ever mention it to you?"

His uncle, a tall, middle-aged man who bore a striking resemblance to his late brother, and to Darcy himself, sat back in his chair and drummed his fingers on the padded arm. They were in the book-room, a space Darcy had always liked, even as a boy when his father would bring him to visit.

"Well, I know your mother favoured the notion of her child marrying her sister's. She and Lady Catherine had a close connexion, as you might recall, despite being so young when she died. I have the impression your aunt has wanted it more fervently since then, to have a stronger tie to her sister."

He had been just thirteen when Lady Anne Darcy had died of infection. Nodding, he said, "But did it go further than that? Did my father ever speak of it to you?"

Frederick shook his head but then furrowed his brow as though trying to remember. "Parents tend to speak of their children, and my brother and I often did. Thus, I suppose I should say yes, but in general terms only. He always said you were too young to make such an important decision—to do it wisely, that is. From what I recall, he planned to have a more serious conversation about marriage and your future duties at Pemberley once you were five-and-twenty. That would be a good age for you to take on part of his work, just as he did for our father, and to start looking about you for an appropriate wife." He gave Darcy a sad smile. "How I wish he had lived that long, as I know you and Georgiana both do. What I know with absolute certainty is that he would want you to do what would bring you the most satisfaction in life. Within reason, of course. Tell me about this young lady you are so fond of and that your mother's people find so objectionable."

"I assure you, there is *nothing* objectionable about Elizabeth," Darcy said. It was an effort not to sound as vexed as he felt; his uncle did not deserve it. His question was understandable and natural. He paused and composed himself before continuing. "Without wishing to sound like a love-sick puppy, I do not see how anyone could find the least thing objectionable about her apart from lacking fortune and connexions. She is a gentleman's daughter," he added and proceeded to provide as accurate a portrait of Elizabeth and her family as possible.

His uncle listened attentively, and once Darcy was finished, said, "I cannot say what my brother would have thought of the situation, but he would judge your Miss

Elizabeth Bennet based on *her* not just her circumstances. It would be preferable if her mother's people were better situated, but you said the uncle who lives in town is respectable, which is comforting. For my part, and I know I speak for my wife and children, we trust your opinion and only want you to be happy. I am willing to speak to her father to assure him we would welcome her into the family."

"Thank you, sir. I appreciate it." This task done, Darcy's mind was already drifting to what else he wanted to accomplish that day.

Showing he had guessed as much, Frederick said, "I am sure you have many other tasks to see to. How long will you be in town?"

"I hope to leave on Monday." He would go to Rosings first, to have a serious conversation with his aunt, one that might result in a permanent breach between them.

"Good. I shall not keep you then, but only if you promise to bring Georgiana to dinner before you go. That way you can see your aunt and Rebecca."

They agreed on a day, and Darcy went to his next appointment.

The Romsleys insisted he and Georgiana spend Sunday with them. It suited Darcy well, as it provided him an opportunity to speak to both his uncle and aunt. As he had with Frederick Darcy, he explained everything he had learnt from his investigations and encouraged the earl to recall exactly what his father had said to him about the future, setting aside Lady Catherine's claims.

"You must know that I intend to explain to Mr Bennet everything I have done and heard, none of which leads me to believe I would honour my father's, or my mother's, wishes by marrying Anne. Lady Catherine says she has letters and an unsigned contract, but have you seen them?"

The earl shook his head, his demeanour reluctant and slightly abashed—although the latter might have been only what Darcy thought his uncle should feel.

Darcy nodded once in satisfaction. "With respect, I do not believe she *can* produce such documents. If there is not even a hint of their existence amongst my father's records..."

"My sister probably...exaggerated, shall we say?" Lord Romsley said.

Again, Darcy nodded. "I shall explain this all to Mr Bennet and ask for his consent to marry Elizabeth. If necessary, I shall share it with every person I know, even those merely interested, should anyone claim I am obligated to Anne. I am not, not by honour and certainly not legally. I will not be prevented from living according to my own wishes by threats, no matter who issues them."

Lord Romsley sighed and scratched a spot above his left eye, only responding after an annoyingly long pause. Lady Romsley smiled kindly at Darcy then watched her husband, allowing him time to reflect on his response. Darcy was glad his uncle did not appear willing to argue with him, unlike when they had been in Hertfordshire, and hoped it meant they would soon settle the matter and forget about it. *Forgetting might not be so easy,* he thought, *but in time, we shall, and as long as Elizabeth is treated as she ought to be, I shall forgive him and my aunt.* It was doubtful his connexion to Lady Catherine would recover; if it survived at all, Darcy would henceforth treat her and Anne as a familial responsibility and no more—one he acknowledged only because he knew it would have pleased his mother.

"Your father talked of it being a good thing," the earl said. "He did, truly. It is the rare man who does not care about expanding his wealth and influence, and Rosings would make a substantial addition to the Darcy fortune and provide a second son with an enviable inheritance. And you cannot overlook that my sisters *did* speak of it as a fond wish." He waggled a finger at Darcy. "Do not mistake that. Your mother wanted you to marry Anne."

"And, as much as I regret it, my mother died when I was only thirteen and Anne eleven," Darcy interjected. "You cannot say that she would want it now, were she still living. Especially if she knew I did not."

"You know she would not," the countess said, speaking to the earl.

Lord Romsley sighed again, this time more heavily. "I suppose. I have thought of the conversations your father and I had often this past week, and, before you ask, as I can see you mean to, he never said he would insist on it. Even when we were your age, he believed young men and women should be allowed to choose their own partners in life. As long as they were making prudent decisions, that is."

Darcy was sitting on the edge of his chair. His uncle's final words brought a scowl to his face. "Please, spare me a lecture on why you do not believe Elizabeth is a wise choice. I know what you would say."

"Do you?" His uncle laughed as though having won a point, which Darcy found puzzling until he explained, regarding Lady Romsley fondly. "You have not yet heard what my wife has to say. She tells me I have changed my opinion and have no objections to the young lady."

Darcy gaped at them, certain he looked as stupid as he felt.

"I have been to Hertfordshire to see your Miss Elizabeth," the countess announced.

Alarm shot through Darcy at the notion that yet another aunt had confronted her. It was soon eased by recalling the earl's final words and continued to lighten as he took in Lady Romsley's smiling visage as she told him of her visit.

"She is a charming young woman," she said. "Intelligent and lively, just as you assured us. Her manners need a little polish, but that is easily tended to, not to turn her into a copy of every other lady of the *ton* but just enough to ensure she earns acceptance. She is caring too. That was obvious in how she spoke of her family, and I would be very glad to know that you and Georgiana had someone who would dedicate herself to your well-being."

"In short," the earl said, "she has convinced my wife that you ought to marry and all without saying a word about it, from what I have been told." He and the countess exchanged a look. "And I realise I owe you an apology. You know how infrequently and reluctantly I admit to being mistaken, but when it is warranted, I shall. I listened to Catherine too readily, and I believed her that you were acting recklessly. I ought to have made my own enquiries, starting by speaking to you. I do *not* agree that I should keep my opinions regarding your life to myself. I am your uncle—"

"And I shall always listen to your perspective and advice, even if I decide not to follow it," Darcy interjected, agreeing with his uncle's sentiment but also wanting to make it clear that he would not be ordered about by anyone.

"As I said to Miss Elizabeth, you are part of this family, thus what you do does affect us," the countess said. "By the same token, how we act has consequences for you. It is worth bearing that in mind."

Lord Romsley and Darcy both nodded.

"Unfortunately, no one can completely control Catherine, and she will be furious, but I shall use what influence I have," the earl said. "As to you, Darcy, I shall say nothing more about who should become the future Mrs Darcy. That is a matter for you to determine. Well, I *will* say that Miss Elizabeth will be received by us just as she would be had she fifty thousand and a dozen dukes for uncles—"

"No one has a dozen dukes for uncles," Lady Romsley said, rolling her eyes.

"I thought you would appreciate my show of good

humour," his lordship said. "Just two days ago, you accused me of being too dour."

They debated the matter for a moment longer, and despite wanting to return to the subject of his future, Darcy left them to it. The couple had been married for over thirty years, and he took their connexion as an example of the one he wished to have with Elizabeth. That summer, he realised that Mr and Mrs Gardiner also had the sort of relationship he wished to have with his wife—one of mutual companionship, respect, affection, love, and friendship. When his aunt and uncle recalled that he was there, they spoke a little more of his current circumstances and his intention to go to Kent the next day, after which he would return to Hertfordshire. The countess assured him that the earl would write two letters for him to bring with him—one for Lady Catherine and the other for Mr Bennet. Both would state that Darcy was under no obligation to Anne de Bourgh, was free to marry where he liked, and that he and his wife greatly anticipated welcoming Miss Elizabeth Bennet as their new niece.

"I shall ensure he does the thing right," Lady Romsley told him.

"And I shall ensure my sister knows that if she embroils me in such a pointless task again, I shall never forgive her," Lord Romsley muttered. "Given I have been called upon to completely revise my opinion in less than a fortnight, I must ask, what was it all for?"

To make me become the only man in the kingdom willing to propose to the same lady three times, Darcy silently quipped. Only for Elizabeth would he be willing to humble himself thus. Soon they would have their reward for how tumultuous their path to happiness had been. Before Christmas, they might be married—would be, if he had his way. All the strife and sorrow of the past year, especially those related to his ill-fated proposal at Easter and her younger sister's elopement, would be forgot, washed away by the joy of being married to the woman he loved more than he had known it possible to love anyone.

CHAPTER TWELVE

Leaving Georgiana with a promise to write as soon as he had secured Elizabeth's acceptance of his proposal and Mr Bennet's consent, Darcy travelled to Kent Monday morning. He would not remain at Rosings long, but he was determined that he and Lady Catherine would understand each other fully before he departed. Never again would either of them speak of her desire that he marry Anne or her insistence that his parents likewise wanted it. If possible, he would forget the events of the past fortnight, apart from a few happy moments, walking with Elizabeth and knowing she returned his love most of all. But there were others, such as Georgiana praising Elizabeth and her eagerness at the prospect of having her for a sister, or Lady Romsley's decision to go to Hertfordshire to know Elizabeth better. Darcy had long thought that his family would love her once they knew her, and his aunt had demonstrated that he was correct. He would add Lord Romsley's apology and that most of his relations were pleased for him and anticipated meeting the lady who had so thoroughly captured his heart.

But nothing will convince Lady Catherine to be reasonable. I must prepare myself for that, he reflected as he gazed out of the carriage window during the drive to Kent. As enraged as he was with her, under the ugly emotion lay sadness. He accepted that today might mark the end of his connexion to his aunt. For his mother's sake, he regretted it; it might also cause uneasy moments with his other relations—Lord Romsley in particular—but there was no avoiding it. *And if the worst happens, the fault will be hers alone.* He was willing to overlook her recent horrible behaviour and even the cruel words she had said about Elizabeth—provided she apologise sincerely to her, him, and others, such as Bingley for dragging his family to Netherfield. He doubted she would be willing to do so.

Having informed her to expect him, Lady Catherine and Anne were awaiting him in the formal, ornately decorated drawing room. Anne watched him warily; Lady Catherine triumphantly.

"You have come to your senses at last," his aunt announced. "I knew you would. I suppose my brother performed his duty and told you it was past time that you did *yours*. He ought to have done so when we were in Hertfordshire rather than permit you to go to Derbyshire. *If* you did."

Darcy remained standing, despite her indicating the chair she wished him to take, which was directly across from hers. "I said I was going to Pemberley and so I did. I am not and have never been a liar, madam, and I resent you implying otherwise."

"You have behaved foolishly, nearly unforgivably, over this business with Elizabeth Bennet," she said, almost as if that gave her permission to insult him. "However, Anne and I shall forget it, now that you are finally prepared to—"

"Let me be very clear, Lady Catherine," he interjected. "I am not here to fulfil the hopes you have so often expressed, which have been nothing but that—*your* hopes, not my obligations." She spluttered, but before she could form words, he went on. "I have come to, once and for all, state that I will *never* marry my cousin. There is nothing to support your claims that you and my father were preparing for me to take such a step, nothing to support that he intended to tell me it was his wish that I do so. In addition, I have consulted solicitors and a bishop, who all agree that I would not be legally bound to marry Anne even if a contract existed, and you, Anne, and I—the ones most concerned in this question—all know that I am not honour-bound to her either. I have always maintained my opposition to the notion, and if you say otherwise, *you* will be the liar, madam."

Her face turned red, while Anne's lost what little colour it had. "I will ruin you!" Lady Catherine threatened. "No one will agree to be introduced to Elizabeth Bennet, let alone befriend her."

Making sure she saw him, Darcy rolled his eyes and shook his head dismissively. "You might make the attempt, but you will fail, especially since your brother and sister-in-law are prepared to embrace her as my wife, as are my father's relations. The only one of us whose reputation will be in tatters is you." He sat and spoke less harshly, knowing this was the final moment when their connexion might be salvaged. "Lady Catherine, Aunt, I knew my father better than you did, knew what kind of father he was. I know without the slightest doubt that if I told him I was adamantly opposed to marrying my cousin and that my reasons were just—that I would never feel for her anything approaching what a man should for his wife, what he did for my mother, and, even more importantly, that I would not be happy with her—he would not have raised the matter again. A choice is before you. You can reconcile yourself to my marriage to Elizabeth Bennet, welcome her as a niece and treat her with all the deference and kindness due to Mrs Darcy, or our connexion is at an end forever. You will not see me or Georgiana again, and we will not write to you. Anne may make her own decision in this regard, if she is willing to defy you." He glanced at his cousin; she was watching him, her expression unreadable.

His aunt's complexion became almost purple, but he thought he saw panic beneath her outward show of indignation.

She said, "You would forbid my niece, my sister's daughter, to—"

"Georgiana asked me to tell you this of her own volition," he said, refusing to allow her to begin a long-winded lecture. "She approves of Elizabeth and my wish to marry her. In her own words, she longs to have her as a sister and, because she cares about my well-being, would rejoice to know that I have a lady by my side who will bring joy to my life. You have lost, my lady. Now that they have had time to reflect, the earl accepts that my father did *not* intend for me to marry Anne and that I have a right to make my own decisions. Further, the countess went to Elizabeth expressly to know her better, and she likes and approves of her. I was with them both just yesterday, and they have promised to welcome my wife into the family. Your brother gave me a letter for you." He took it from his jacket pocket and held it out to her. "I suggest you read it carefully and consider what I said. I shall go for a walk and return in one hour. You have that long to decide what you will do."

Darcy stood and left the room; neither lady spoke as he did, but as soon as the heavy wooden door was closed, he heard his aunt's strident voice. During the interval he had granted her, he strolled through the grounds, revisiting some of the paths he and Elizabeth had taken earlier in the year. His thoughts were heavy, and the weight of them slowed his steps and kept his head lowered. What would his aunt do? Would his mother have been bitterly disappointed by how he was treating her sister?

Soon, his reflections turned to a more pleasant subject: Elizabeth. How they had misunderstood each other! One day, he would learn to laugh about it. She would tease him into doing so, and he would love every moment of it. He had changed a great deal in the last half year—for the better and thanks to her. Tomorrow, their life together would finally begin. Provided there were no more obstacles, that was, and he was prepared to tear and kick them all to pieces, just as he had spent the last week doing to Lady Catherine's last attempt to force him into a life he had never desired.

"I shall be with you soon, my love," he whispered, the image of Elizabeth in his mind. For a time, he stood in a grove, leaning against an old oak tree, and contemplated the wildness that surrounded him. He had seen Elizabeth in a similar repose. She had once claimed it calmed and even soothed her if she forgot everything and focused only on the sights and sounds of nature. At present, doing so allowed him to come to terms with the situation with Lady Catherine and release part of the simmering anger he felt towards Lord and Lady Romsley for having accompanied her to Hertfordshire. That freed yet more space in his mind and heart to experience the up-lifting sensation of his love for Elizabeth.

"Tomorrow, my darling," he said. "Tomorrow."

CHAPTER THIRTEEN

Although the distance between Rosings and Longbourn was not especially long, by the time Darcy left, it was too late to safely complete the journey. He went as far as possible before stopping at an inn. It meant he arrived rather earlier than he otherwise would have, had he set out from Kent this morning.

As much as he longed to see Elizabeth, his first conversation must be with her father. The aged butler showed him to the gentleman's book-room. Mr Bennet regarded him, his brow arched high, holding a cup in one hand and remaining silent until the servant closed the door.

"Well, this is a surprise," he said. "Perhaps not to see you, but at such an early hour. I must say, Mr Darcy, I had more or less anticipated you would call last week or whenever it was I told Elizabeth she must send you on your way, to allow you to marry your cousin and keep your fine relations content. And, most importantly, away from my family."

Darcy stood by the door. It took effort not to retort, but nothing would be served by antagonising the older gentleman. "I did not think there would be much purpose. From what your daughter said, your mind was firm. Therefore, I used my time and energy on altering my circumstances, doing what I could to address your concerns."

"Did you?" Mr Bennet seemed amused. He waved towards a chair. "Do sit. I shall injure my neck if I keep looking up at you."

Before complying, Darcy pulled three letters from his pocket and laid them on the desk. "You will find in those proof that I am not engaged to my cousin and neither does my family expect me to marry her and, further, that they would welcome having Miss Elizabeth as part of our family. Most of them, I should say. Regrettably, Lady Catherine prefers to maintain her stubborn, irrational opposition to the notion that I am an independent gentleman with the rights that affords me, including most notably the decision of whom I shall marry. I have broken with her. My sister and I shall not see her or communicate with her again. Your daughter will never have to be in company with her, and, on her own, there is nothing Lady Catherine can do to harm her or me in society or amongst my relations."

"Oh? Your relations, you say? You are aware that Lizzy received a visit from a countess late last week?" He sipped from the cup and placed it on the desk, but he did not reach for the letters.

"I am. Lady Romsley likes Miss Elizabeth. Both she and my uncle Romsley anticipate introducing her to our social sphere, and my aunt has promised to assist her in establishing herself in her new role in life."

"Supposing you propose, she accepts, and I give my consent," Mr Bennet said. It was not a question.

Swallowing his irritation, Darcy said, "One of the letters I brought is from Lord Romsley. The other is from my father's younger brother, assuring you that he, too, has no objections. Both men are also familiar with my father's thoughts on the matter, and I believe they wrote of it. The final missive is from my solicitor, confirming there is no existing contract or other obligation existing between me and my cousin Miss de Bourgh." He leant forward, erasing a small portion of the distance between them. "Sir, I am not and have never been engaged to my cousin. I am *not* bound by honour to her. Lady Catherine would like me to marry her daughter based on day-dreams she and my late mother had when we were infants. In short, I am at complete liberty to give my heart and my hand to whichever lady I like, and the one I like—the one I *love*—is your daughter Elizabeth. She told me she disclosed the whole of our connexion to you. Thus, you know I have loved her and desired to make her my wife for months. My feelings go back to when I was here last autumn, and she captured me with her fine eyes, wit, liveliness, and…and…"

"That is quite enough of that." Mr Bennet sat up in

his chair, let out a loud gush of air, and reached for the letters. Staring at them, but not breaking the seals, he said, "No man really wishes to hear another speak of being in love with his daughter. You will understand if *you* are ever the one sitting behind a desk." He returned the papers to the table and rested his hands on top of them. "Your uncles are fully aware of Lizzy's circumstances, her lack of dowry and my wife's connexion to trade?"

"They are. While they would prefer it if the latter were not true, it makes little difference to them. In the end, the Philipses and Gardiners will be my new family, not theirs, and I was pleased to assure them that your brothers- and sisters-in-law are respectable people with excellent characters. The money can be of no concern to anyone but me, and I have sufficient wealth. I do not know how Lady Catherine learnt of your youngest daughter's elopement and subsequent marriage, but she did inform the earl and countess. Since the couple *are* married and few know the whole tale of their union, it, too, is easily overlooked."

Apparently, Elizabeth had not told her father that Darcy knew of the elopement, and they spent several minutes discussing it. Suspecting it was best to be as open as possible with Mr Bennet, and hoping it would improve the gentleman's opinion of him, Darcy disclosed that he had found the couple and convinced Wickham to marry the girl.

Mr Bennet removed his glasses and rubbed his eyes. "Well, that is...I suppose I should thank you, and when I am less shocked, I shall. I pray you never know what it is like to confront the truth that you have failed your child. When I believed my brother Gardiner had done the business, it was difficult enough, but that you—" He sighed and ran both hands over his face before meeting Darcy's eye, his emotions under regulation once again. "For now, I shall show my gratitude by telling you to go find Lizzy and say what you will. You have my consent." Impatiently, he waved a hand, sending Darcy away.

Darcy was out the door and down the stairs before either of them had time to draw breath.

Elizabeth was chatting with Jane and Mary in the drawing room, their mother and younger sister having their own conversation, when the door suddenly flew open. Surprised, all sound immediately ceased, and she was sure more than she looked to see who had entered with such haste; how could they not?

It was Mr Darcy. Her Mr Darcy had finally returned! Relief flooded her, leaving her heated and lightheaded. She smiled, likely the largest grin she had ever made, and she drank in the sight of him, watching as his eyes scanned the occupants until his gaze fell on her.

Without looking at her mother, he said, speaking rapidly, "Mrs Bennet, I humbly request a private interview with Miss Elizabeth. She might like to—"

"Take a walk," Elizabeth interjected as she leapt to her feet. "I would," she added, feeling breathless and on the verge of bursting into happy tears. It was all she could do not to shout that yes, she would marry him even though he had not yet proposed. Not today, that was.

"Mr Darcy?" her mother said. "Lizzy, what are you doing? What is happening? I do not understand."

"Everything is as it ought to be," Jane said, her tone calm. "I shall explain. Mr Darcy, it is *very* good to see you again. Enjoy your walk, Lizzy."

Elizabeth, who had paused some half a dozen feet from Mr Darcy when her mother said her name, nodded at her elder sister, and, glancing at the gentleman, directed him from the room. She walked towards the rear door that opened to the gardens.

"You need a coat," Mr Darcy said.

"Do you really wish to wait five or ten minutes while I find one?" she asked, sounding as astonished as she felt.

Fortunately, there was no need to debate the matter. The butler ambled towards them, holding her dark blue spencer.

"Here you are, Miss Lizzy," he said, his voice raspy with age.

"Thank you." She accepted the garment, looking the old man in the eye and, as she did at least once a day, said, "You need to retire. You know there is a snug cottage waiting for you on the estate."

"When you and your sisters are all married," he said, a small smile on his lips; his eyes flickered towards Mr Darcy.

Elizabeth chuckled and continued towards the door as she donned her jacket. "It is our joke," she explained.

"He has served at Longbourn since my great-grandfather's time. He only works an hour or two a day now, but he will not give it up."

As soon as they were outside, she stopped and regarded him, her eyes wide and tapping one foot. She was both impatient and anxious, a tiny part of her still unwilling to give up the fear that their story would not end well, despite her best efforts to banish it.

He said, "I love that you care for an old servant's well-being, that you treat him and everyone else you encounter with kindness and consideration. I have missed and dreamt of seeing your beautiful face since the moment we parted."

She felt herself blush and shyly averted her eyes. Taking his hand, she said, "Come, let us move away from the house. I suspect more than one person will watch us from the windows if we do not."

It seemed he would not release her hand, even if she had attempted to free it, and, taking quick, long steps, they were soon in the copse and hidden by trees, many of which were still largely full of leaves.

When they stood still, he pulled her hands to his mouth and kissed them. "Please, forgive me for not saying whatever I should, given we have not seen each other in over a week, but, for what I believe is the third time, Miss Elizabeth Bennet, you must allow me to tell you how deeply, truly, unendingly I love you. I beg you to relieve my suffering and consent to be my wife."

She laughed—how could she not?—and cried, "Yes, oh yes, of course I shall!" Suddenly, it seemed like it was the brightest, warmest, most beautiful spring day—a time for rejoicing and new beginnings—not the damp, cool autumn day it was, one that evoked shivers and thoughts of the long darkness of winter.

Mr Darcy—finally truly *her* Mr Darcy—expressed himself as well and as sensibly as a man violently in love possibly could, and she was not at all dissatisfied with the passion of his embrace. She had never been kissed in such a manner, and, as she rested her head against his broad, firm chest, listening to his heart and enjoying the unimaginable comfort of his arms wrapped around her body, she sighed, releasing all the vexation and anxiety she had experienced since his last ill-fated proposal; indeed, it seemed that every moment of unease she had ever had in her life vanished at once.

"Have you suffered terribly while we were apart?" she said.

"Very much so. I did not know what and how long it would take to convince my uncles or your father to accept our marriage, if I would be able to at all. In the end, the business was done as easily and quickly as I suppose was reasonable." He spoke for a few minutes of his time at Pemberley and his conversations with Lord and Lady Romsley, Mr Frederick Darcy, and, just that morning, her father.

"Ah, Lady Romsley," she said. "I believe I shall like her best of all your relations, apart from you and Miss Darcy. Her visit gave me hope that she and others would not think so poorly of me, once they got over their shock that you would marry the penniless daughter of a country gentleman."

"She likes you very much. But why are we speaking of anyone other than us?"

Tilting her chin up, she silently asked for a kiss, which he provided. She then said, "I am afraid we must, but not for much longer. Dare I ask about Lady Catherine?"

He shook his head. "I no longer consider her a person I need concern myself with. I shall tell you everything, but not at this moment, if you please."

Standing on the tips of her toes, she kissed him this time, rather than wait for him to kiss her. "I am content to set aside talk of other matters for now. Later, we might tell each other in excruciating detail exactly what we did and felt during this separation. Oh, I hope we shall not have another for a very long time!"

"I do not intend that we shall. If possible, I would take you away immediately, some place I would not need to share you with even one other person."

Joy bubbled up within her and, yet again, she smiled and laughed. "I do love you so very much. I would happily follow your plan, but I think Papa will insist we are married before he allows you to carry me off. And, on that score..."

"Tell me we shall be married before Christmas," he implored.

She nodded, her grin momentarily preventing her from speaking. "If you agree, Jane and I have it all arranged. Mr Bingley knows, as well, and thinks it the most excellent notion. We shall have a double wedding at the start of December. Do you see? Even when I was afraid to believe everything might turn out as it should, even when I said those hurtful words to you—which I did not want to do, I only did because—"

"I know, my love, and I understand. I am also choosing to accept that your father behaved sensibly, all things considered."

"I did not give up hope, not in my heart," she said. "Whether that is because I am stubborn or simply because I know there would be no real happiness for me without you, I cannot say."

Her darling betrothed rested his forehead lightly against hers and whispered, "I feel the same. My life would be poorer without you in it. Colourless. I could never have given up fighting for us, not when I knew you returned my love."

Then, looking into his dark eyes as he lowered his lips towards hers yet again, she reflected that *this* was their true moment of happiness—made all the sweeter for having been in doubt—one that promised the most wonderful, perfect future anyone could ever imagine possible.

ALSO BY LUCY MARIN

A Matter of Prudence

A Pinch of Salt

Being Mrs Darcy

Christmas at Blackthorn Manor

Darcy and the Blue Devils

Her Sisterly Love

His Family Objects

The Marriage Bargain

Mr Darcy: A Man with a Plan

Mr Darcy's Second Chance

Mrs Bennet Makes a Match

The Art of Apology

The Recovery of Fitzwilliam Darcy

The Truth About Family

Whoever Lives in Love

Paperbacks Available in Large Print Format

A Matter of Prudence

Being Mrs Darcy

The Marriage Bargain

Anthologies & Collections

'Tis the Season

Happily Ever After with Mr Darcy

Mr Darcy's Second Chance

Prudent Arrangements

The Family Circle

ABOUT THE AUTHOR

Lucy Marin developed a love for reading at a young age and whiled away many hours imagining how stories might continue or what would happen if there was a change in the circumstances faced by the protagonists. After reading her first Austen novel, a lifelong ardent admiration was born. Lucy was introduced to the world of Austen variations after stumbling across one at a used bookstore while on holiday in London. This led to the discovery of the online world of Jane Austen Fan Fiction and, soon after, she picked up her pen and began to transfer the stories in her head to paper.

Lucy lives in Toronto, Canada, surrounded by hundreds of books and a loving family. She teaches environmental studies, loves animals and trees and exploring the world around her.

SCAN HERE
to go to
Lucy Marin's books on
Amazon

GET A FREE BOOK!

The Course of True Love, a contemporary Pride & Prejudice variation is free for subscribers of the Quills & Quartos newsletter. CLICK HERE to join us today!

Cover image shown is a vector based depiction of a man and a woman embracing with a sketch of London behind them.

ACKNOWLEDGMENTS

My thanks to Amy, Jan, and the rest of the Quills & Quartos team, and to my family for supporting my writing habit.

Manufactured by Amazon.ca
Bolton, ON

58895813R00096